Siberian slaughter

"Son of a bitch!" Barrabas snarled, jumping down from the cab roof and sprinting for the fallen figure of Billy Two.

The Russian MG crew was waiting for something just like that.

Slugs cut a line of death at Barrabas's heels, forcing him to turn away, to turn back. "Bastards!" he raged.

Liam O'Toole dived at his leader, hitting him behind the knees, knocking him down as more bullets tracked his torso.

'Get off me, O'Toole!" Barrabas yelled. He stared across the ice at Billy Two. "Nobody gets left behind," he shouted. "Nobody *alive*."

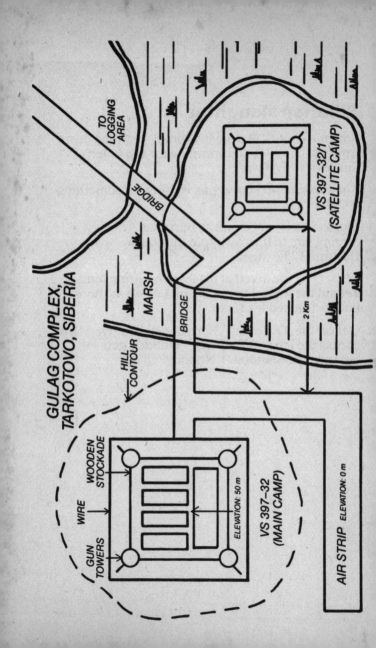

GULAG COMPLEX, TARKOTOVO, SIBERIA

TO LOGGING AREA

BRIDGE

VS 397-32/1 (SATELLITE CAMP)

MARSH

BRIDGE

2 Km

HILL CONTOUR

WOODEN STOCKADE

WIRE

GUN TOWERS

ELEVATION: 50 m

VS 397-32 (MAIN CAMP)

AIR STRIP ELEVATION: 0 m

SOBs
GULAG WAR
JACK HILD

A GOLD EAGLE BOOK FROM

W🌐RLDWIDE

TORONTO · NEW YORK · LONDON · PARIS
AMSTERDAM · STOCKHOLM · HAMBURG
ATHENS · MILAN · TOKYO · SYDNEY

First edition March 1985

ISBN 0-373-61605-8

Special thanks and acknowledgment to
Alan Philipson for his contributions to this work.

Printed in Canada

1

Anatoly Leonov shuffled out the camp gates, into the frigid 5:00 A.M. blackness. The collar of his quilted prison jacket was turned up to protect the back of his neck, and a rag muffler triple-wrapped his head from chin to eyes. He was surrounded by a moving mass of similarly bundled human shapes, the men of the *rabskaya sila*, his fellow slaves. They tramped through drifts of new-fallen snow, felt boot soles squeaking on its powdery crust. They marched in silence to the shrill piping of an arctic wind and the steady jingle of the choke chains that connected armed KGB bluecaps and the guard dogs.

Leonov squinted, raising a hand to shield his eyes from wind-driven needles of ice. Beyond the halo of hard white glare thrown by the gatehouse kliegs, beyond the dark expanse of frozen marsh ahead, fairy lights twinkled atop a low hill.

It was VS 397-32, the parent camp.

A painful lump rose in Leonov's throat. On an equally bleak morning two winters before, when Leonov, the renowned research biologist, and his friend, Valentin Vasilyev, had just begun their sentences of ten years at hard labor, Vasilyev had glanced over at the same low glittering hill and growled a single word.

"Xanadu."

In that one word, muttered like a curse, the professor of literature had summed up the smallness of their convict-dreams, the true measure of their degradation. For Vasilyev and Leonov, and the other prisoners condemned to "special regime" camp VS 397-32/1, the "strict regime" colony across the marsh was nothing less than a pleasure dome. The inmates there got Sundays off and meat scraps in their soup twice a week. And they worked only twelve hours a day inside the protection of the compound buildings, making wiring harnesses for small household appliances, such as toasters and electric irons.

Tears flowed freely down Leonov's gray-bearded cheeks. Tears drawn not by the cutting edge of the wind, but by a crushing sense of loss. There would be no more bitter brilliance, no more incisive wit. No more treasured friendship to ease the burden of his imprisonment. Valentin Vasilyev had disappeared the day before. He had gone out with the rest of the logging crew in the morning but had not returned with them at dark.

Leonov knew there was no hope. His friend was dead. Every night, after brutal labor in the forests, the *zeks* trooped gratefully back to their ramshackle prefab cell blocks, their bedbugs, their putrid rations. The squalid prison camp, "Slash One," was their only defense against Siberia, the man killer. Other convicts had disappeared in winters past. Some were never found. Some were discovered after the spring thaw, devoured by wild animals, their splintered bones scattered across the taiga floor.

Like a zombie, Leonov trudged on in the middle of the pack, his tears freezing the rag muffler to his beard. Inside a numbed body, his scientist's mind, trained, rational, deductive, kept shifting through the available facts and coming to the same agonizing conclusion. Vasilyev wasn't a *dokhodyaga*, a "goner." Despite having endured starvation rations and hard labor for more than two years, he had still been in relatively good physical shape. Barring a serious accident, he had certainly been strong enough to walk the four kilometers back to camp with the crew. Leonov had asked questions of the few political prisoners—"prisoners of conscience"—on his friend's work detail. If there had been an accident, none of them would admit it; no one had seen or heard anything. Apparently, while his fellow *zeks* had their backs turned, Vasilyev had slipped quietly off into the snowy forest to sleep. To die.

What hurt Leonov more than the loss of companionship, more than the feeling of being deserted and therefore betrayed, was the thought that their shared confidences, the communication between them, had been superficial. A comforting illusion was shattered. He hadn't known Valentin Vasilyev at all.

The logging crew crossed the ice-bound marsh on a wooden bridgeway without rails, a ten-foot-wide path supported by low stilts. It had been built for summer when the marsh became an impassable, sulphurous bog. They walked close together, a phalanx five abreast with the weaker ones all in front, shielding the stronger from the gusting wind. The guards and dogs brought up the rear. Leonov's position, first row, closest to the right edge of the walkway, was the most exposed of all. It was his not through a lack of strength but a lack of caring; he was lost in memories and grief.

They were halfway across the marsh bridge when something hit Leonov hard behind the right knee. As his leg buckled under him, a shoulder slammed into his left side, butting him off the path. Helpless, he crashed to his back on the frozen mud.

For a moment he lay there stunned, rigid, unable to regain the air that had been knocked from his lungs. As the paralysis faded, he gasped for breath. The sky above him was starless, an oppressive blanket of black. There was no time to survey possible injuries. In a panic, he rolled to his stomach and quickly pushed to his knees, then his feet. His right leg would not support him. He fell again, this time on his face.

Groaning, he clawed himself back up on all fours.

The logging crew had stopped on the walkway, stopped to stare. Their huddled, shadowy forms were backlit by the kliegs of Slash One, the warmth of their breath, of their bodies, turning to shimmering clouds of steam.

No one offered to help him.

The bluecaps shouted for the crew to move on. Because of the knot of men on the bridge, they were unable to see the cause of the delay.

Leonov crawled forward. He had to get back up on the path before the guards pushed through the crowd of prisoners. If he didn't, he would be technically "refusing to work." And the guards, at their own discretion, would be free to turn either the dogs or their AKR assault rifles on him. He dragged himself to the edge of the walkway, then reached up and gripped it with his right hand. At once there was a terrible pressure on his fingers.

A boot.

Leonov writhed but was unable to pull his hand away. He could get no traction on the ice.

"You must be more careful, comrade," a gravelly voice said from above.

The voice and the boot belonged to Kruzhkov, the self-appointed boss of Vasilyev's work detail. The huge, heavyset convicted murderer was a *pridurok*, a trusty. His fellow inmates had other, more accurate names for him, among them "half-breed" and "bitch." In return for certain favors, special privileges, he worked for the gulag guard staff as a camp storm trooper, an unofficial enforcer of unwritten policy. What one *zek* did to another was conveniently beyond the reach of Soviet law. For the small group of prisoners of conscience at Slash One, life under the domination of Kruzhkov and the other hardened criminals was an integral part of their punishment, like exposure to the elements and the endless toil.

"You must be more careful or you're going to have a terrible accident," Kruzhkov said, grinding the heel of his boot down on the trapped fingers, making their joints pop and crack like dry twigs.

Leonov could feel his finger bones separating. He screamed against clenched teeth.

The guards, impatient for the comfort of their heated huts in the logging area, used truncheons and snarling dogs to reach the cause of the tie-up. As the crowd parted for them, Kruzhkov shifted his boot, reached down and grabbed Leonov by the wrist. With one seemingly effortless jerk he hauled the scientist back up on the walkway.

For an instant, Leonov stared straight up into Kruzhkov's face. Above the top of the man's filthy rag muffler, on either side of a bulbous, dripping nose, small dark eyes danced with delight. Before the scientist could fully recover, he was roughly turned and the flat of a broad hand slammed between his shoulder blades, shoving him forward, out of the way. Warily, cradling his bruised hand, Leonov looked back. The murderer-bitch already had his nose in its customary position: pressed firmly between bluecap butt cheeks.

"No problem, sirs," Kruzhkov assured the irritated guards. "The idiot was walking in his sleep. I know just how to wake him up. He can take the place of the man I lost yesterday."

"Move along!" one of the guards ordered. They didn't care which work detail Leonov was part of. All that mattered to them was that the daily quota of felled trees was met. And that nothing drew them from the warmth of their huts until it was time to verify the log count.

"You heard him," Kruzhkov said, giving Leonov another shove. "Move it!"

The biologist limped away, forcing his knee to bend, to bear his weight. Under his breath, he muttered desperate prayers. They were answered. The more steps he took, the easier it became to walk. By the time the prisoners reached the far side of the marsh and the upgrade that led to the timberline, he knew he was going to be all right. For the moment.

Kruzhkov, following hard on his heels, goaded him up the steep, snow-choked road.

"Our famous scientist is a famous fool!" the bitch shouted at Leonov's back, shouted for the other *zeks* to hear. "Sent to vacation with us because he asked too many questions about people who don't matter. Troublemakers. Traitors. After two years, he still hasn't learned to keep his mouth shut. There are still questions he must have answered. Today, famous comrade, your dear friend Kruzhkov is going to teach you the lesson you were sent here to learn.''

Leonov knew better than to respond. To do so was to invite another "accident." Given the living conditions, the cold, and the system, even a minor injury at Slash One could prove fatal. There was no doctor, no nurse, and the only available medicine was aspirin. If a wound was serious enough or became infected to the point where a *zek* could not leave the compound to fulfill his daily work requirement, the staff considered him a "goner" and immediately put him on half rations. The goners were not permitted to return to barracks and bunks after the morning meal. They lay in varying stages of delirium on the floor of the mess hall, drawn to the failing warmth of its wood-burning stove. Some lasted less than a week.

The lucky ones.

Leonov looked at the men around him. Not the thieves and murderers, but the politicals. Brave men who despite the well-advertised risks had repeatedly spoken out against their government's policies. The crusaders for human justice climbed the hill, heads lowered, bellies growling, determined to live through one more day in hell no matter what the cost. They fervently believed that that attitude was all that separated them from the goners. Leonov knew, as had his friend Vasilyev, that there was no distinction. Slash One was a process. It transformed men into animals, animals into stones, stones to animals again. Back and forth, over and over, until the "special regime" was complete, until the will to live was ground away.

As for the criminal majority at Slash One, they had pretty much everything they wanted, everything available given the limits of the camp. They had the freedom to subjugate the prisoners of conscience, to rob them of rations and money, to rape them— there are no women in special-regime camps. They did the least amount of work and never suffered for it in the mess tent because the bitches needed their cooperation to make the system run. The bitches did no physical work at all, except for beatings, and seemed to positively thrive on prison food, their faces plump, bodies filled out. Everyone knew those at the very top of the criminal dung heap were getting supplements on the side. The regular food always left the prisoners of conscience hungrier than before they sat down to eat.

Leonov and the others got their first break of the morning only after the crews reached the end of the road, the logging area. The bluecaps turned on the floodlights and unlocked the tool shed. While the bitches issued saws, chains, axes, the *zeks* stood meekly in a queue. Though their forward progress was stopped, the prisoners continued to move, shifting their weight from one foot to the other, trying to maintain body heat. A conga line of the doomed. The prisoners of conscience were relegated to the very end.

Before Leonov's turn came the bitches ran out of tools. That didn't mean he didn't have to work. Those without tools used what God had given them—hands, backs, legs.

Kruzhkov nodded and smiled at the bluecaps as they headed for their heated huts. Then he snarled, "Traitors, over here!"

The prisoners of conscience assembled in front of him. Eight men counting Leonov.

"You disappointed me yesterday," Kruzhkov said. "I believed in you and you let me down. I lost fifty rubles. Today, with the help of Comrade Leonov, you will succeed. And I'll win back my money with interest. You know what I want to see. Now, get to it!"

Like the others, Leonov looked up at the tall pine tree with dread. It could be done. It had been done before. But not without a price in hours of toil and pain. The *zeks* lined up on one side of the trunk and on the count of three began to push. The branches dropped snow on their heads as the upper part of the tree shuddered from the impact; the base did not move at all. The prisoners quickly changed sides and rammed again on the count. There was no discernible progress, except for the removal of more snow from the high branches. The tree's roots remained locked to the frozen ground. The men switched sides and continued, falling into a steady rhythm.

The Siberian winter sun was at its full height, the light of noon a dim, somber gray before the prisoners were allowed to stop. The snow around the tree trunk had long since turned to mush, the rock-hard earth churned to slippery muck.

Leonov sat in the snow with the others, watching as Kruzhkov surveyed the fruit of their labor. The huge man was not pleased. "At the rate you're going," he said, "it'll be a week before you rock this tree out of the ground. I want it down before evening. And to show you how much confidence I have in you traitors, I'm going to go over to the other detail and double my bets with the crew boss."

The prisoners of conscience said nothing, made no protests; there were no groans. Leonov stared at his boot tops. He wondered if Kruzhkov really had a bet on. He doubted it.

"You, Leonov," the bitch said. "You come with me. It's time for your education. The rest of you, get back to work!"

The biologist got up and fell into step behind Kruzhkov. He was both light-headed and soft in the legs. Not just from the exertions of the morning. His life was in jeopardy.

Instead of heading back to the clearing where the bitches usually built their bonfire, Kruzhkov led him deeper into the virgin forest, along a path Leonov had never traveled. If he was to be punished for asking questions about his friend's disappearance, there would be no fair fight involved—if any contest between a 140-pound undernourished biologist and an experienced heavyweight could be considered fair. Punishment was dealt out by a squad of bitches and thieves. Four or five to hold the victim down, one to do the actual beating.

If I don't struggle, Leonov told himself, if I cry out at every blow, maybe they won't hurt me too badly. Maybe they won't break anything.

Then he smelled the cookfire. The bitches had killed a deer or something and were roasting it far away from the other prisoners, so they wouldn't have to share any of it with the guards.

"Smells good, doesn't it?" Kruzhkov said, stepping aside and making Leonov walk in front. His small dark eyes twinkled. "Tell you what, famous comrade, if you still want some after your lesson, I'll see what I can do about it."

Whatever faint hope the scientist held vanished. They were going to hurt him badly. Very badly. No matter how meekly he submitted.

He pushed aside a pine bough and stepped into the gathering of murderers and thieves. Seated on logs ringing a roaring fire, they were drinking moonshine and watching their dinner cook.

The joint of meat was unidentifiable. A charred, sizzling mass skewered on a wooden spit.

Leonov had been two years without fresh meat. His mouth flooded with saliva. It was not the reaction of an educated man; it was the reaction of a dog.

Kruzhkov's hand clamped down on the biologist's shoulder. "Look, there," he said, pointing up in the trees on the other side of the fire.

At first Leonov couldn't make it out. Something hanging from a large branch. The carcass of the animal they were eating. Then the smoke and waves of heat shifted and Leonov could see. It hung by one leg. The other leg was gone, hacked away at the hip socket.

It had not occurred to him that Kruzhkov was going to answer his questions. Or that the answer he sought could be worse than any he had imagined.

"Hungry?" Kruzhkov asked.

Appetite had turned to horror. It was Valentin in the tree, upside down, naked, his throat slashed. Ruby icicles hung from the tips of his hair.

Horror turned to rage.

Even as Anatoly Leonov snatched up a stout length of limb from the heap beside the fire, he knew he was doing just what they wanted him to. He knew and he didn't give a damn. He swung the branch with all his might. There was real power behind the blow, the power of a peaceful man's fury, but it was poorly aimed.

Kruzhkov grunted as the branch smashed against his broad chest. Stunned by the force of the impact, he staggered back a step, tripped over the pile of firewood, and twisting as he fell, landed face first.

Leonov tried to follow up his advantage, jumping forward, club raised high over his head. Before he could deliver another blow, the other bitches jumped him, disarming him and fighting him to the ground.

"Kill him! Kill him, Kruzhkov!" they shouted as the big man scrambled out of the wood pile.

Arms and legs pinned to the snow, Leonov watched Kruzhkov carefully wipe the blood oozing from his nostrils on his jacket sleeve.

"Go on, kill him!" the criminals cried impatiently.

Kruzhkov smiled. "Too easy," he said, stepping up to the defenseless man. "Too quick."

The kick slammed into Leonov's side. Something snapped in his chest. A rib. Then two more savage kicks in exactly the same spot. The biologist could not even scream for the pain.

The kicks stopped but the agony continued, as did the chorus of shouting.

"More! Stomp him!"

"If you don't want to smash his head in, we'll do it!"

"No!" Kruzhkov growled, waving them off. "If he's killed now, he gives us no sport."

Leonov blinked up at the huge man leaning over him. Kruzhkov's muffler had slipped down to his chin. There was fresh blood smeared all over the lower half of his face; it was on his teeth as well. The biologist sipped at the air, unable to draw a full breath for the pain in his chest.

"Comrades," Kruzhkov said, as much to Leonov as to the others, "I'm taking bets on how many days it will take for this traitor to die."

2

Walker Jessup popped the cold salmon canapé into his mouth, crunching the crisp, coarse flatbread square, the translucent pink curl of Swedish gravlax and dollop of sour cream with such fervor that it set his chins quivering. Even as he tipped the fluted tulip glass to his lips, rinsing his palate with crackling cold champagne, his free hand hovered over the vast silver hors d'oeuvre platter, moist fingertips poised.

The firm white flesh of Indian Ocean prawns lured him. As did little tubes of rare roast beef rolled tightly around a chive-and-cream-cheese stuffing. But his hand returned again to the beluga. Rounds of thin toast piled high with chopped hard-boiled egg and onion and topped with a glistening black crown of caviar. A weakness of his, certainly. Perhaps even a fault of character. Jessup could not leave them alone. They disappeared into his mouth at such a furious pace that finally he had to stop to catch his breath. Even as he gasped, his eyes stayed locked on the remaining half-dozen beluga canapés.

"More, sir?" the liveried buffet attendant asked.

It was not a polite offer of service; it was an expression of sheer disbelief.

Jessup blinked at the servant, then surveyed the huge oval tray. A tornado had struck the three meticulously arranged, concentric rings of tidbits. And the remaining six caviar morsels sat alone, huddled, waiting for the end. The big Texan was sorely tempted to put them out of their misery, but the sight of the devastation he alone had wrought gave him pause.

Some people drink to avoid unpleasant realities, some take refuge in wild sex binges, others consume vast quantities of food. Although Walker Jessup dabbled in all three traditional escape routes, he was first and foremost an eater. That coupled with the genetic curse of a slothlike metabolism kept his average weight in the neighborhood of three hundred pounds. Currently, it was closer to 350. What he saw on the platter before him was irrefutable evidence of his mental state. The former CIA operative was sick at heart. It had nothing to do with the approaching Christmas holidays; it was purely a job-related depression.

Jessup shook his head at the attendant. "No more," he said. He drained his glass of champagne. It was only then that he noticed the other party guests, waiting impatiently with plates in hand, unable to get at the hors d'oeuvres because of the immovable obstacle in the middle of the serving line. A mountain in a size sixty-two black tux. As Jessup moved out of the way, they swarmed in to fill the vacuum.

Through the ornately draped windows of the banquet hall, he could see a light snow falling. Inside the Georgetown mansion everything was warm, snug and festive. And why the hell not? The federal legislature was in recess. And the veteran senator who owned the mansion was in a unique position. He had one more year of free ride before he had to run for reelection. And that reelection was one hundred percent guaranteed.

Jessup couldn't stall the inevitable any longer. He lumbered out into the crowded foyer where he spotted the senator's wife in an animated conversation with two other ladies. Three parakeets in prom dresses, all in their sixties.

"Excuse me, ma'am," the Texan said in a somber drawl, "but is your husband around? I'd like a private word with him, if I might."

The woman squinted up at him for a full ten seconds, teetering slightly on her high heels, then exclaimed, "Why, I know you! You're Mr. Fix-it. Girls, this is Mr. Fix-it."

Her announcement caused giggles all around.

The parakeets were plastered.

Walker Jessup was not "Mr. Fix-it." In the highest echelons of power on Capitol Hill he was known as "The Fixer," a man who ran his own private intelligence service, with connections in mercenary and criminal undergrounds, and who, for the right price, could arrange for anything to happen.

Anything, anywhere.

"Your husband, ma'am," Jessup prodded gently.

The petite woman gave him an irritated look, then said, "I believe he's in the library. Going over something or other with his secretary."

"Thank you," the Texan said, nodding to the matrons.

The one with silver-blue hair batted false eyelashes at him over the rim of her champagne glass. A serious come-hither look. Jessup stifled a shudder, managed a noncommittal wince and beat a hasty retreat.

He rapped lightly on one of the library's double doors. Over the noise of the party, the music, the laughter, he thought he heard a reply, so he turned the brass knob and slipped inside.

In the book-lined room there were two leather upholstered couches, an armchair and an enormous desk. A leggy brunet, the senator's new secretary, leaned against the front edge of the desk, an expression of all-consuming boredom on her pretty face. The senator sat in front of her in his motorized wheelchair. Only the back of his balding head was visible. His face was buried to the ears in bosom. Bare and ample bosom.

The brunet gave a little start when she saw Jessup step into the room. The briefest flicker of surprise.

Then, coolly, firmly, she pushed the legislator out of her cleavage. As she shrugged back into the straps of her evening gown, the old man spluttered a feeble protest. The brunet nodded toward the door. "Your nine-o'clock appointment is here, sir," she said.

The senator snapped his head around, flinching at the imposing height and bulk behind him.

"The rewards of public service, eh?" Jessup said, fighting hopelessly against the broad smile smearing over his face, transforming it into a smirk of grandiose proportions.

"I'll leave you gentlemen to your business," the brunet announced, deftly zipping up the back of her dress. She didn't concede a goddamn thing. Not embarrassment. Not guilt. She stepped around Jessup like he was a piece of oversized, overstuffed furniture, her perfect turned-up nose pointed at the ceiling, her rounded hips swinging in a tight, controlled arc.

"I should've gone into politics," Jessup muttered as he watched her exit.

"Lock the doors," the senator said.

As Jessup complied, the old man added icily to his back, "I trust what you just saw will go no further than this room."

"Not to worry. In my book every man has a right to a hobby."

The lawmaker shot him a milk-curdling look. "Sit down," he said, pointing toward a narrow armchair.

Way too narrow.

Jessup lowered his robust backside onto one of the couches instead.

The legislator snapped his wheelchair into gear. It lurched across the Persian carpet with a shrill whine, stopping just short of Jessup's toes. "The committee is anxious for a progress report," the elder statesman said, his hand firmly gripping the throttle lever. "Let's have it."

Jessup's black mood returned with a vengeance. As far as he was concerned the senator had always been a pompous, double-dealing little hypocrite. Now he was all of the above...on wheels. And a national hero to boot. The much-heralded sole survivor of "Jonestown II," as the electronic media called it, found among the heaped and bloated dead of a Honduran killer cult by the boys with the body bags and the hankies tied over their noses. For sticking his grubby little fingers in the wrong slice of the Central American pie, the senator got his spine snapped, but he was too mean to die. Regrettably, he remained Jessup's only link with the mysterious "committee."

His extensive intelligence network notwithstanding, Jessup knew more about who didn't sit on the committee than who did. It wasn't an official Senate or governmental body, but tax dollars secretly funded its works. The best-spent money in the budget, to the Texan's way of thinking. And not just because it kept him in caviar.

The committee was a star chamber. A righteous kicker of deserving and overdue asses.

Independent of constitutional checks and balances, of the restrictions of international treaties and law, it applied surgical military solutions to specific and longstanding problems. Solutions too dirty for the Armed Forces, for CIA or its surrogates to touch. Too dirty and too dangerous.

The current project was no exception. In scale, however, it blew all past escapades out of the water. In scale and risk. It was the latter that weighed so heavily on Jessup's mind. Risk had been part of all the covert operations he had organized over the years, from Vietnam to the present. But even in the most chancy of those there had always been a clear line between winning and losing; cross over and the danger ended. In this mission no such line existed.

"We are still set for the twenty-third, weather and unknowns permitting," Jessup said flatly.

"Excellent! Then we should have him to safety by Christmas Day."

Safely in front of the TV cameras, Jessup thought sourly. The rouged, Pan-Caked, electronic likeness of Anatoly Leonov would sweep across the free world's boob tubes, bumping regularly scheduled programming to deliver the teleprompter's carefully constructed message.

It was all show biz.

And nobody on either side of the iron curtain, nobody pulling the strings, gave a damn about

Anatoly Leonov, the man. The Soviet scientist had become a living symbol to both East and West. As a symbol of dissent he had been sentenced to hard labor in Siberia; as a symbol he would be rescued. He was a treasured object to be hoarded, controlled by the most powerful. And if a great man can be reduced to thing status, what about the anonymous soldiers-for-hire who put their lives on the line to serve him?

Tools.

Replaceable parts.

The senator beamed at him. "To snatch a prize like Leonov from inside the USSR. This is the dirty trick to end all."

It was more than that, and they both knew it. It was the unthinkable, the undoable. Nobody broke into Siberia. And sure as hell nobody ever broke out.

"If that robber Barrabas and his band of degenerates pull this one out of the hat," the senator continued, "it will have been worth every dime they gouged us for."

Jessup idly scratched his topmost chin. This mission was big money, all right. Seven figures per man over expenses, with half up front. The senator had, true to form, haggled about the outlay, but his heart hadn't been in it. For him the deal was a bargain at twice the price. A bargain if Barrabas and his SOBs managed to free the prisoner and clear Soviet airspace. Or if they died trying.

The senator couldn't lose on this one. Success would produce a mother lode of international publicity, part of which he would certainly find a way to lay claim to. Failure would vindicate his long-standing public position on the "immorality" of covert action. It was a position he gave lip service to because it got him votes. The lawmaker's only firmly held belief was unspoken, yet a matter of record: he would do anything to stay in office.

Failure of the mission had another bright spot for him. It would destroy a group of men he thoroughly despised because they possessed skill and attributes he did not, skills and attributes that had indirectly cost him the use of his legs. Nile Barrabas and his SOBs had butchered and bagged the private army of one of the senator's longtime secret financial supporters, an American expatriate in Honduras who was a cross between Jim Jones and Charles Manson. The senator had had the misfortune to be in the same room with his old buddy when the bad news arrived about the five-hundred-man assault force. The senator's forte was conventional diplomacy, country-club deals struck in smoke-filled backrooms, and every time that tried-and-true approach failed, every time he had to surrender the baton to the bigger, the stronger, the braver, he lost a little bit of his own painstakingly accumulated power. For the senator, giving up the use of his legs was nothing compared to giving up personal clout on the Hill. The former could be turned to advantage; the latter was defeat. Total defeat.

"GRU isn't having any second thoughts, I trust?" the old man said.

Jessup shook his head.

Nobody broke into Siberia. Entry was by invitation only. In this case, by invitation of *Glavnoye Razvedyvatelnoye Upravleniye*, Soviet Military Intelligence, "weak sister" to KGB, tasked with the collection of strategic, tactical and military intelligence, conduct of guerrilla warfare and industrial espionage.

"That part of it has gone down exactly as we hoped," the fat man said. "GRU is so eager for the goods, they've put their own butts on the line to get it. They had to guarantee the SOBs' good conduct before KGB would agree to let them into Russia."

"The SOBs' 'good conduct'!" the senator exclaimed, then laughed a dry, brittle laugh. "Oh, that's marvelous, just marvelous!"

Jessup said nothing. It wasn't marvelous. It was only logical. With the right bait there was no such thing as a closed door.

"And Cruikshank? Is he under control?"

The fat man shifted his bulk on the couch. The rescue plan had been complicated and dangerous enough without the insertion of J. Cruikshank into the works. Cruikshank was a Silicon Valley entrepreneur who had missed the gold ring. A loser surrounded by legions of winners. An egomaniac.

He had acquired the trappings of success, the requisite red Ferrari, Lear jet, yacht, but it was all a colossal, credit-financed front. Unable to keep up with the younger, brighter competition, he had switched leagues...and games. Twice he had been implicated in the sale of prohibited high-tech hardware to the Soviets. Nothing had ever been proven.

It was another of Cruikshank's illicit goodies that GRU was currently thirsting after: a redesigned processor board for an IBM mainframe computer. The Soviets weren't supposed to have the mainframe, either. It had mysteriously disappeared from a customs warehouse in Switzerland and resurfaced two months later in a tank factory east of the Urals. The new add-on processor board would almost double the speed performance of the mainframe and increase substantially the automated plant's production of T-72 tanks.

"The son of a bitch insists on being present at all negotiations," Jessup said. "That's created problems because of the CIA and State Department surveillance he's under. It's conceivable that the interference of our own people could compromise the mission."

The senator shrugged.

"Somebody from CIA or State could step into a bullet."

"We can't have it any other way. It's got to be business as usual. Hardball. The Soviets have got to think we don't want them to have the goods and that we'll do anything to keep them from getting it."

Jessup didn't need the logistics of the job explained to him. "I've got no problem with doing what has to be done in the field," he said tightly. "Just as long as I'm not the one who has to break the news to the widows and orphans."

The senator smiled.

He wouldn't be breaking any bad news, either.

"I'll relay your report to the committee," the legislator said, glancing meaningfully at his wristwatch. The audience was over.

Jessup rose and headed for the door.

"Send my secretary in," the senator said to his broad back.

The fat man didn't respond with a customary surly wisecrack; he didn't even slow down. He stepped out into the foyer, past the waiting brunet, without uttering a word. And made a beeline for the hors d'oeuvres.

In his absence the buffet table had been completely restocked. The other guests around the food had no choice but to give him ground. It was either that or be trod upon. He grabbed a fistful of beluga canapés and began to toss them into his mouth like kernels of popcorn.

Responsibility hung heavy on his soul as he mechanically chewed and swallowed. He wished to hell he hadn't offered Barrabas the rescue job in the first place. He wished to hell Barrabas had turned it down. But all the wishing in the world couldn't change the way they were. It was in Jessup's nature to organize the impossible; in Barrabas's to attempt it. The risk of this mission didn't end when and if the SOBs broke through Soviet border defenses to the West. In order to free Anatoly Leonov they were pulling a royal double cross on GRU.

GRU didn't recognize borders.

And it never forgave, never forgot.

3

Erika Dykstra shut the lid of her packed suitcase and looked up from the brass bed on which it sat. Across the room her lover stood in front of the narrow windows, tall, straight, unmoving. The corded muscles of his triceps bulged the sleeves of his gray T-shirt as he stared down three stories to the tiny, snow-choked courtyard of her eighteenth-century Amsterdam house. Stared without seeing.

Too well she knew that expression, the cold distant look in his heavy-lidded eyes. She knew and hated it. Nile Barrabas was no longer hers. He was swept up in the details of the upcoming mission, rerunning the assault plan over and over in his mind, attacking it from every conceivable angle, looking for unseen weak points, inventorying countermoves.

For almost ten years, since the last days in Vietnam, their relationship had been going on. On and off. Whenever the white-haired mercenary found himself between wars, healing up, he sought out her company. Until it was time to fight again. The worst of it for her wasn't the string of goodbyes or even his months-long absences. It was feeling him gradually pull away from her, losing him to the mission; it was having him there in the flesh but not in spirit during their final days together. It almost made her hate him, almost made her wish he was really gone. It certainly made her want to cry, but she did not.

Erika Dykstra was an extraordinary woman. She and her brother Gunther jointly ran a family corporation, Netherlands Imports Management, an international concern that for five generations had moved rare commodities, art, gold, gems, in a duty-free, tax-free environment. The beautiful, statuesque blond smuggler could have had practically any man she wanted. It did not escape her sense of the ironic that the man she had finally chosen was the one she could never possess.

Hard winter sunlight, reflected from steep, snow-covered neighboring roofs, undercut the stark planes of Barrabas's face, the jutting cheekbones, brow and chin. That face never failed to move her. It was not actor-handsome or male-model-handsome. His features weren't finely drawn; they were, in fact, rather brutal. It was the totality of the face, the raw power and determination, the character it radiated, that attracted women like moths to the proverbial flame. In the beginning, Erika, too, had thought of him as the ultimate challenge to her feminine wiles. But very soon she had realized it was a game she could not win. He was already married, wedded till death to his violent profession. If she wanted Nile Barrabas, it had to be on his terms, not hers.

Moreover, she had to accept the fact that in his great strength, his skill as a warrior, was a terrible weakness. A fatal flaw. Strength has no value unless it is applied. Tested. Erika's lover was addicted to the test. The risk of his own life. He thrived on the adrenaline fix only a firefight could provide.

Out of all the missions over the years, all the godforsaken hell holes, the filthy forgotten places, the current job was unique. Barrabas had never been secretive about his work. Not with her. Not before this. And never had he asked her to pack up and leave her home, to go halfway around the world, to hide in anticipation of something he was about to do.

"Don't ask," he had said.

A simple demand. It had chilled her to the bone. Whatever the new mission was, it was no limited, Third World conflict, no hit and run, somebody else's disaster to be neatly left behind. This one was going to bring the roof down.

She crossed the room and stepped behind him. As she reached up to touch the back of his head, to stroke his thick mane of silver hair, she paused. Her hand began to tremble, and there was a sharp, building pain in her throat. She had said goodbye forever to this man so many times before and every time, no matter what the odds, he had returned to her. Despite herself, though she knew very well the dangers of his profession, in her heart she had come to expect the impossible of him, to expect him to always come back. She could see the rise and fall of his back and rib cage as he breathed, the twitching of the tension-knotted muscles in his arms. He was mortal. Mortals fell in battle. Suddenly it was like the first goodbye forever all over again. I will not make a scene, she told herself, swallowing her anguish. I don't want him to remember me that way.

"Nile," she said softly, slipping her hands around his lean, hard waist.

He did not flinch at her touch. "Ready?"

"Uh-huh." She tried to lock him in an embrace, but he twisted free, turning to face her.

"You tell the Amirthalingams hello for me," Barrabas said. "Tell them that I miss them all."

"Of course." Erika was leaving Amsterdam for Bombay, to stay with longtime friends and business associates. To submerge. To disappear.

He looked into her blue eyes and read her concern. "It's going to be all right. Everything's going to be all right. I'll send word when things settle down. We'll meet someplace exotic and primitive. Fiji, maybe. How's that sound?"

"It sounds fine." A single burning tear rolled down her cheek.

Barrabas pulled her into his arms and gently kissed her.

"Let's get you to the airport," he said.

NILE BARRABAS sipped from the thimble-sized cup of triple-strength coffee, then dragged deeply on his half-smoked cigar. Except for the proprietor, a wizened little old man in a stained white apron who sat reading a Dutch newspaper behind the service counter, Barrabas had the coffeehouse all to himself. It was a tiny oasis in the middle of the flesh-and-vice supermarket of Walletjes, Amsterdam's redlight district. A rudimentary oasis. The booth Barrabas occupied had no cushions, just cramped plywood seats permanently attached to the wall. He could barely see through the fogged-up windows beside the booth. The snow in the gutters had turned to slush, tinted hot pink, then blue, then hot pink again by the flashing marquee of the "Gay Cinema" three doors down.

The white-haired man sent a plume of Havana smoke aloft, eyes closed, lost in thought.

He didn't pay attention when the doorbell jangled, signaling a new customer had entered. When the newcomer took a seat opposite him in the small booth, he paid attention.

"Say, man," the uninvited guest began, leaning across the table, "how'd you like to buy some hashish?"

Barrabas chewed the butt of his stogie, sizing up

the guy grinning at him. He was in his late twenties, had a floppy-rimmed leather hat, a greasy beard and a fringed suede jacket, likewise lubricated. In his right ear was a small gold earring.

"It's great stuff, and I'll give you a good price."

"Not interested," Barrabas said.

"A chick, then?" the pusher continued undaunted. "I know this thirteen-year-old who can suck the brass off a . . . ."

"You a registered voter?"

The question stopped the pusher-pimp cold.

"Are you registered to vote, yes or no?" Barrabas repeated.

"Yeah, sure. A registered Socialist. What's it to you, man?"

"Reassurance," Barrabas said, staring into yellow-tinged, bloodshot brown eyes. The theory of a participatory democracy was indeed wonderful. Every man as informed decision maker. Rule by reason. The reality was something considerably less attractive. Appealing only when compared to the authoritarian alternatives on the left and right. Barrabas no longer fought for political systems, in principle or in practice. He fought for money. Sometimes he fought for friends. In the case of the Soviet dissident, it was neither. He didn't need the money and he didn't know Anatoly Leonov. He knew of him, though. Everyone knew of him. Outside Barrabas's coterie of mercenaries very few men had his unqualified respect. Though he and the imprisoned scientist were opposites in many ways, opponents in method and philosophy, the soldier of fortune respected the man of peace. A warrior is not measured by the caliber and quality of his weapons but by what he makes them do. Anatoly Leonov had crossed the line his country had scratched in the dirt, knowing he would lose, that he had to lose. He had not stepped over in anticipation of prizes, adoration, a place in the history books, but because he had to, for himself.

For the same reason, precisely, Nile Barrabas had agreed to try and free him.

"How 'bout the chick?"

The white-haired man pulled the cigar from his mouth and gestured toward the door with it. "Out, citizen," he said.

The registered voter registered no protest. There were ambulances in his tablemate's eyes. Ambulances and stretchers and intensive-care wards. All for him. The pusher-pimp slipped away on tiptoe. Quietly. The bell jingled once as the door opened and closed.

Barrabas cast his mind ahead, beyond the mission at hand, trying to see the future. His future. As always, there was nothing to see. Only impenetrable blackness and, he fancied, the faint, yet unmistakable stink of brimstone. He smiled and puffed his cigar.

"Who the fuck wants to live forever?" he asked the man behind the counter.

The aged proprietor lowered his paper. "Only a fool," he said.

Barrabas nodded. "Only a fool."

4

Major Yevgeny Grabischenko, deputy chief of GRU, reached out a pudgy hand for the brimful tumbler of vodka. In a single, smooth motion, he raised the glass from table to lips, and with a practiced flip of the wrist, tossed the liquor down his throat. He slammed the tumbler back to the table top.

"Thirteen!" he said through clenched teeth.

Across from him sat an equally porcine man in a three-piece Brooks Brothers suit. Viktor Volkopyalov, one of the many deputy heads of KGB, grabbed the bottle of imported Polish spirits by the neck and sloshed his own glass full. Volkopyalov had a very florid complexion and a potatolike nose with impossibly tiny slits for nostrils. He was a confirmed mouth breather. "You can't win, you know," he said, holding the tumbler to the light, admiring the oily sheen of its contents. "You are not in my league. Never were, never will be."

Grabischenko's stomach tightened as his former friend did in the ounce of Wodka Wyborowa, then smacked his lips appreciatively. Drink for drink, that was the name of the game. Until one of them threw in the towel, threw up or passed out. It was a game they had played as KGB recruits, a test of strength, manhood, a bond of comradeship. Now, it was merely an exhibition of one-sided power, domination.

"You never win," Volkopyalov gloated.

"To the motherland!" Grabischenko said, gulping another measure of pure grain spirits. The booze burned deep in his guts, as did the truth of Volkopyalov's statement. "Fourteen!" he said, slamming the glass down.

The KGB deputy head helped himself to another shot, evening the score, then thumbed back the sleeve of his suit jacket, exposing the crystal face of a Rolex Oyster. "We now wait the traditional ten minutes, unless you wish to concede the contest."

"Of course not," the GRU man snapped. The ten minutes between rounds was the wickedest part of the drinking bout. It allowed the alcohol already downed to work its way into their bloodstreams.

Grabischenko pushed back in his chair, stretching his short, stout legs, and surveyed the cut red velvet wallpaper, the faceted glass baubles hanging from the chandelier. A private room in a private Moscow club. No spectators. The game had changed from a joyous celebration of youth and high spirits, a public celebration, to a somber battle of wills. A trickle of sweat oozed down his right cheek, down the heavy folds of flesh between his jaw and shirt collar. Aside from the vodka flush, he felt all right. Moments before the contest had begun he had slipped out and guzzled a half-liter of vegetable oil. That fluid protected him, lubricating his stomach against the fire of the hundred-proof, easing the way for the evening's inevitable climax.

"I hope your American gangsters don't embarrass you," Volkopyalov said. The lie rolled easily from his tongue. "Or if they do, that the advanced technology is worth the destruction of your career."

Grabischenko shifted on his chair. He said nothing. They both knew that the Cruikshank processor board was at the top of the five-hundred-page "requirements list" put out by VPK, the fourteen-member Military-Industrial Commission supervising all defense-related production in the USSR. The processor board, unlike most of the forbidden items on the list, was without a price tag. That meant it was to be obtained at any cost, monetary or human.

"You have read their dossiers, I trust?" Volkopyalov said.

"In detail."

"What beauties GRU is sponsoring! Killers for hire. Professional hooligans. To allow even one of them into our country is a risk. To allow six in borders on the criminal."

It was a point that had been brought up countless times in the preceding weeks. Grabischenko's answer was, accordingly, well rehearsed.

"Installing the processor board in an existing plant is a complicated procedure," he said. "It must be tested, calibrated, tuned. Our people in Ust Tavda are unfamiliar with the refined technology. We are confident the black marketeers will give us much more than just the add-on board. They will show us how to adapt and apply it to other plants."

"I hope you are just as confident that you will be able to keep them under control."

"They will be under constant surveillance and armed guard by GRU's finest the entire time they are here."

Volkopyalov gave him a bored look, then checked his Rolex. He smiled craftily. "Time to resume," he said, pouring vodka for the both of them. "I'm thirsty, aren't you?"

Grabischenko picked up his glass.

"To your continued excellent health!" Volkopyalov said in a voice dripping with sarcasm.

The GRU deputy chief emptied his glass. "Again," he said, holding the tumbler out. His lips and nose were numb. Soon the sensation, or lack of same, would creep upward, into his brain. He had already passed his body's alcohol limit, but it was too late to back out. He had to play the game through to the finish. Though it galled him no end, it was more in his interest, in GRU's interest, for him to lose to Volkopyalov than to beat him. It was a way of confirming the established pecking order. The more confident the KGB man was in his power, professional and personal, the more likely he was to underestimate his enemy.

Though Grabischenko had started out in KGB, his allegiance had changed radically when he had been appointed to a top post in Military Intelligence. His job was to compete with the stronger bureaucracy. It was a contest stacked against him from the start. That he had made a modest success of the task had made him many foes in his old branch of the service. One of them was Viktor Volkopyalov.

The KGB deputy head gulped his twentieth shot with a flourish, grinning at the full glass in Grabischenko's hand. "Had enough? Do you surrender, comrade?"

The GRU man's head was reeling, his stomach churning. The smug look on Volkopyalov's ruddy face gave him a surge of fresh determination. He got the tumbler to his lips, but no farther. He could not drink it.

Growling a curse, he threw the glass aside, lurching up from the table, staggering for the door and the lavatory beyond. Behind him, Volkopyalov roared with drunken glee. He couldn't make it to the door, let alone the men's room. Grabischenko fell to his knees before a potted palm, shoving his head in among the sharp green fronds.

"The pride of the GRU!" Volkopyalov croaked.

Grabischenko was rackingly sick, but the vegetable oil did its job, easing the sudden transition from full stomach to empty one. For a moment at least, his head cleared. He straightened up, mopping his mouth with his handkerchief, then stumbled for the door.

Outside he staggered into the arms of a waiting GRU captain. Through the open door behind them, they could hear the laughter of Volkopyalov. "Balandin," Grabischenko said to the captain, "get me out of here."

The tall dark officer helped him down the hall and out the front steps to his limousine. The cold night air slammed into Grabischenko's face, beating back the waves of nausea. He stared into the hard, level gaze of Captain Balandin and felt a sudden rush of drunken sentimentality. Balandin was like a son to him. Loyal. Dedicated. A credit to the GRU organization. Quite literally the best it had to offer. Over and over he had proven himself worthy of the deputy chief's ultimate trust. Grabischenko sucked in the frigid breeze; it felt like razor blades sliding into his nostrils, filling his lungs. It sobered him momentarily.

"We must be careful," he said as the younger man guided him into the limousine's back seat. "KGB wants us to fail. That's the only reason they've allowed the operation to go this far. They want to embarrass GRU and weaken it permanently. If we succeed, of course, it will have the opposite effect."

Balandin took a seat beside his superior. A confident smile played across his mouth. "Then we must succeed, sir. At all costs."

Grabischenko nodded. And was instantly sorry. The abrupt head movement and the close, stifling quarters of the limousine brought back his nausea. He lowered his power window and thrust his head out not a second too soon.

5

Claude Hayes's head hit the headliner as the speeding Sno-Cat bounced over a shallowly buried boulder and veered hard right. "Christ! Take it easy, Billy!" he said to the huge, half-Osage, half-Navaho Indian hunched over the steering wheel. "You're gonna put us in a goddamn ditch!"

"I never figured you for an old woman, Hayes," the red man said, swerving left to miss an exposed outcrop.

Hayes groaned as he was slammed into the passenger door. He wasn't an old woman. He was a former Navy SEAL, a freedom fighter alongside his black brothers in Africa. He was not averse to risking his own life. He just didn't like risking it for no damn good reason. "Slow down!"

"Easy, buddy," Billy Two said. "It's just around the bend up there. See that smoke up ahead? That's from his cabin."

Hayes glared out the windshield. He liked Africa. Alaska he purely hated. It was cold as hell, and there was depressing snow everywhere.

"This guy had better be good," he said sourly.

Billy Two laughed. "Chank Dayo is the best. Best bush pilot. Best scout in the Alaska National Guard. Hell of a kickass in a tight spot, too."

"I never met an Eskimo before."

"They're just like everybody else. Love to have fun. Drink. Screw around." Billy Two gave his traveling companion a sly look. "And it's true what they say about 'Eskimo hospitality.'"

"What's true? What're you talking about?"

"You must've heard the stories. You know, Eskimo pappy shares Eskimo mammy with honored guests from the south."

"Bullshit!"

"Hey, if you don't want your share, just leave it to me, buddy. I know just what to do with it."

Hayes returned the Indian's sly look. "I take it you've been up here before?"

Billy Two grinned. "Her name is Noweena. She is one female in a million. Untamed. Hayes, you're going to fall in love."

"And your pal, he doesn't mind?"

"Like I said, it's an ancient custom."

Hayes crossed his long legs and laced his fingers behind his head and the hood of his parka. "When in Fairbanks..." he said.

They approached the cabin. It was a small place, made half of stone, half of timber, with a steep roof. It was surrounded by pine trees. Everything was covered with a couple of feet of snow, but a path had been shoveled from the front of the cabin around the side. Billy Two parked the Sno-Cat and they got out.

"Go on," he said to Hayes, "knock on the door. Noweena might have a little surprise for you. She's been known to run around the cabin with no clothes on."

Hayes frowned. William Starfoot II was a renowned joker and jerk-off. The story he was telling was getting a bit too good to be true. He had to admit, though, his interest was sorely peaked.

He rapped on the wooden front door. It wasn't locked. The pressure of his knocking opened it inward. It was light inside and warm. But there was a peculiar smell. It made Hayes wrinkle up his nose.

"No-wee-na!" Billy Two called sweetly over his shoulder.

Like magic she appeared. All seven feet and one thousand pounds of her. Noweena stood on her back legs, her huge paws stretching out for the black man's head, her muzzle dripping, her foul garbage-pail breath gusting into his face.

Claude Hayes was a seasoned warrior, not one to panic. What immediately followed was not panic, exactly. More like a temporary inability to accurately measure the severity of a threat. He had never been nose to nose with an Alaskan brown bear before.

"Ki-aiiii!" he shouted, lashing out with a savage front kick that landed amidst the bear's breadbasket.

"No, you dumb bastard! No!" Billy Two howled.

He wasn't the only one howling. Noweena, her dignity ruffled, her home invaded, let out a thunderous bellow of rage and charged.

Hayes and Billy Two ran for their lives. They sprinted twice around the perimeter of the cabin before Billy Two scrambled up the woodpile and onto the roof. Hayes followed on his heels, dragging himself up to the roof's peak.

"Oh, shit," he groaned. "It's coming up after us!"

Indeed, the bear was trying to climb the woodpile to get at them, but the quartered logs kept slipping under her great weight.

"Chank's got to be around here," Billy Two said.

"What's that little shack over there?" Hayes asked, pointing. "There's smoke coming out of it."

"It's a steam hut," Billy Two said. "He's got to be in there." He cupped his hands and hollered, "Chank, help!"

"Help!" Hayes echoed. Then he yelled at his Indian guide. "You asshole, why didn't you tell me she was bear?"

"She's a bear," Billy Two said.

Eight-inch, razor-sharp talons were methodically splintering the edge of the roof.

"And there's one other thing I forgot to mention...."

Hayes scowled at him.

"You never kick a bear."

THE SWEAT POURED OFF the stout, hairless body of Chank Dayo in a torrent, pooling on the rock floor on which he squatted nude, barefoot, eyes shut tight. The *qasegig*, or sweat hut, was an integral part of traditional Eskimo culture, a meeting place, social center. This particular sweat hut was Chank Dayo's private refuge. The place where he divested himself of the residue of the white man's poisons he so dearly loved: bourbon and perfumed women.

This was no ordinary sweat-it-out session. He had come off the preceding six-day drunk seeing visions. Not pink seals or lavender walruses. But visions of his own death. So real, so intense that it had scared the hell out of him. It wasn't just the seeing, either. It was the feeling.

As he squatted there, heart pounding, the vision replayed for the hundredth time.

His view of the death scene came from a position above and some distance away from his physical body. It was as if his observing spirit floated, not free but tethered by sensation to the brown man running up a frozen slope above an airstrip. Running. Hearing shouts he did not understand. Those dream shouts were so loud, so real they almost made him open his eyes. Then the heavy machine gun opened fire; he was hit and he fell. His spirit returned to his pain-twisted body. As he lay on his back he saw a plane flying over, felt its prop wash, then he was inside the plane looking down at his dying body, watching it grow smaller and smaller until it vanished.

Chank opened his eyes and blinked rapidly, shaking his head to clear it. He was by birth an Inuit. The Inuit believe that a man's soul upon his death is immediately transferred to another body. There is no heaven, no hell, no true death; only instantaneous transformation. The circumstances of his birth notwithstanding, Chank Dayo was a creature of the twentieth century. A Marine veteran of Vietnam, much decorated. A hotshot oil-company bush pilot. A freelance fuck-up and whore chaser. The only part of the old ways he believed in was the bit about there being no chiefs and no gods.

As a twentieth-century man, he didn't like visions. Especially ones without unclad females. Ones in which he could feel the bullet impacts, slugs slamming into his legs. Visions without hope.

He tossed another clump of old rubber snowmobile tracks into the fifty-five gallon drum that served as his steam hut's heating unit. Sweat out the booze, he told himself, sweat out the booze and you'll be okay.

The shouting continued. He listened to it closely for the first time. They were coming from outside. He rose from his squatting position and kicked the door open. His plump seallike body steaming, Chank Dayo stepped naked out of the hut. When he saw his pet bear and the two men she had trapped on the cabin roof, he forgot his troubling premonition.

"Chank! It's me, Billy Two!" shouted one of the frantically waving men. "Call off the bear!"

The Inuit held his hand to his forehead, squinting against the glare of sun on snow.

"Chank, call off the goddamn bear!"

Dayo put his hand to his mouth, cupping it like a megaphone. "You been molesting my old lady again, Starfoot?" he cackled.

6

The red-haired man entered the posh lobby of Garlowe Publications, Inc., and walked straight up to the receptionist's desk.

"Yes, may I help you?" the buxom fifty-year-old receptionist asked in her best Bronx-robot voice.

"My name's Liam O'Toole. I've got an appointment to see Alfred Lord Garlowe. It's about my poetry. I submitted some to him."

"You're a poet?" she said doubtfully, looking at his stocky, powerful frame, meaty forearms and wrists, and thighs that stretched his khaki slacks to the near-splitting point.

"A battlefield poet," he said.

"Oh, *that* O'Toole," she said. "Yes, of course, Lord Garlowe is expecting you. It's the double doors at the end of the hall. I'll tell him that you're here. Go right in."

O'Toole fought the urge to sprint the length of the hallway. His heart thumping, he strode the deep pile carpet. More than anything, Liam wanted to be published before he perished. Now someone was actually interested in his work. Given the nature of the mission on the front burner for him and the SOBs, it was none too soon. Along the walls were framed covers from Garlowe, Inc. books. He glanced at the titles as he walked. Curiously enough, there didn't seem to be any poetry. A lot of how-to books, though. How to play with yourself. How to play with somebody else. And books on currently popular medical topics such as AIDS and herpes, books on life after death and astrology. Maybe Lord Garlowe was just starting to get into poetry publishing? Whatever, O'Toole thought, the big man at a New York house had read his stuff and had liked it well enough to call him in for a conference.

Nothing was going to spoil his day.

O'Toole opened the doors without knocking and entered. The president and publisher's suite was vast, wall-to-wall bookshelves and sweeping Manhattan view. Liam was met by a very tiny man with a cold hand.

"I'm Lord Garlowe," the little guy said, giving him a broad and highly artificial grin. "And this is Malcolm Strangways."

The other occupant of the suite was standing in front of the wet bar, a tall whiskey and soda in his fist. He raised his glass to O'Toole in salute, then half drained it in a single go. He was dressed in Gucci paratrooper boots, a camouflage jump suit by Givenchy. There were heavy gold link bracelets around both his wrists and in his other hand was a massive black briar pipe.

"Come in and have a seat," Lord Garlowe said. "What's with you, Strangways? For God's sake, get the man a drink."

"Irish, neat, if you've got it," O'Toole said.

"You know of Mr. Strangways, of course," the tiny man said as he rounded his enormous Danish modern desk. He disappeared for a moment, then reappeared on the leather-upholstered executive swivel chair.

O'Toole wondered if he used a kiddy seat. He was so distracted by this possibility that he failed to answer Lord Garlowe's question.

It was repeated.

"A poet?" O'Toole said, making a wild stab.

Strangways chuckled melodically as he handed Liam his drink. "A poet and a prophet both," he said.

O'Toole found himself staring at Strangways's nose. Under a pink-colored substance, like makeup, it was beet red. The substance was peeling off in little flakes. Some of them floated in his whiskey and soda. It didn't seem to bother Strangways.

"No, Mr. O'Toole," the president and publisher corrected, "Mr. Strangways is a world-renowned author."

"I write the famous Obliterator series," the author announced. He chuckled some more.

Liam gave the tiny man a helpless look.

"Blood and guts," the lord said. "Action and adventure for men."

"Sorry, I've never heard of it. I don't read much fiction." O'Toole drank some Bushmill's.

"I've taken the liberty of showing Mr. Strangways your war poetry and he was very impressed."

"Very," said the author.

O'Toole positively beamed. "Thank you both. My work all comes from actual incidents. Things I've lived through, guys I've known over the years. When do you think you might want to publish it?"

There was a sudden silence in the suite.

"You do want to publish it, don't you?"

"Not exactly," the lord said.

O'Toole's beam winked out.

"You see," the tiny man went on, "Garlowe, Inc. publishes the Obliterator. And Mr. Strangways is currently in need of a research assistant."

Something had, indeed, spoiled Liam's day.

"You're offering me a desk job?"

"Not exactly."

"What we'd like," Strangways butted in, "is to have you help me write future sequels to my series. Give me authentic detail, true grit. You know."

"Maybe if you saw one of his books," Lord Garlowe said, sliding a slim paperback volume across the teak desk top.

"That's the Obliterator on the cover," Strangways told him. "A hero in ten languages."

O'Toole looked at the portrait of the bare-chested blond man in mortal combat and laughed aloud.

"What's funny?" Strangways asked.

"The hero's got his hammer on half-cock," Liam said. "A .45 won't shoot on half-cock. The bad guy's got him dead in the water."

O'Toole opened the book and skimmed a page or two, flipped to a new chapter and skimmed some more. Again, he broke out laughing. When he looked up, both publisher and world-renowned author were glaring at him. Figuring that another explanation was in order, he explained. "This reads like it was written by a chimpanzee."

The glaring got even more intense.

Liam walked over to the bar and refilled his glass. "You've got some real problems with your product," he told them.

"That's what we need you for," the lord said. "To straighten the little problems out, to give it some punch. I'm sure we can come to some equitable financial arrangement."

"I thought you wanted to publish my poems."

"That is a very real possibility," Garlowe said. "A very real *future* possibility. Right now, the market for poetry books is too weak to consider it."

O'Toole emptied his glass.

"We're ready to talk terms, contracts," Strangways assured him.

"Frankly, gentlemen, I don't need the money," Liam told them. "And I don't think my putting in the right details is going to make your books any better. You see, I come from the you-can't-write-it-if-you-haven't-lived-it school of literature. And I get the distinct impression Mr. Strangways hasn't been there."

"You're refusing?" the lord said.

"I'll tell you what," O'Toole said, a wicked gleam in his eye, "it just so happens that I know of an expeditionary force leaving the States in a couple of days to fight insurgents in the Horn of Africa. A real war. Real bullets. Real blood and guts splattered all over the place. I can arrange for Mr. Strangways to go along if he wants to. He can see it all firsthand. Write the truth, write from life."

Strangways visibly recoiled.

As O'Toole figured he would. The red-haired man poured the last of the Bushmill's into his glass, filling it almost to overflowing. "My offer is going..." he said, pausing to take a long pull on the Irish. "Going..." He paused again, drinking deeper, draining the glass. "Gone!"

Publisher and world-renowned author exchanged looks of disgust.

O'Toole dropped the empty bottle into the wastepaper basket and headed for the door. He opened it, then turned to deliver his parting shot. "But if you ever need somebody to do further research for a sequel to *Sixty Ways to Choke Your Gopher*, you got my number."

ALEX "THE GREEK" NANOS rose shakily from the king-size bed. Across the room, through the open bathroom door, he could see Sunny, the light of his life, showering. Her perfect, all-over tan was partially obscured by the dappling on the shower-stall glass. Even so, the sight of her au naturel gave him a telltale and agonizing throb. She had the power to do that. To raise him from the dead and gone with a single sidelong glance.

The man who looked back at him from the mirror over the bureau was a sorry sucker. Thin. Not weak, but the bulk of his weight-lifter's muscles, the hard bulges of lats and delts, the powerful ribbing of abs had shrunk away.

Nanos was wasting away and loving every minute of it.

He'd talked Sunny into giving up her career as a topless-bottomless dancer in San Francisco's North Beach. His passionate Greek blood couldn't handle the idea of other guys...and broads...drooling over his love mate. There was turnabout, though. Sunny had agreed to give up her career, only if Nanos would give up his.

It was harder than Nanos figured.

He had to choose between the two ultimate male macho fantasies. The one about the older stud and the young blonde who worships the ground he walks on. And the one about being a soldier of fortune, rootless, ruthless and highly paid.

Nanos looked down at himself. He was rubbed red and raw from friction. Sex was great, even when it hurt. It hurt all the time, now. He shuffled into the bathroom and stood by the shower. Now that he was closer, he could see her much better through the distorted glass. The result was more than a mere throb.

He groaned.

"Alex?" she said over the hiss of the shower. "My folks are coming over tonight. That's all right with you, isn't it?"

The Greek winced. There were some drawbacks to playing house with a girl who might have been his daughter. Two specific drawbacks came immediately to mind. Sunny was a California girl, born and raised. Her parents were Midwestern transplants, roughly the same age as Nanos. They had very different attitudes, however. They were practicing nudists, pacifists, vegetarians. The Greek was uneasy about public nudity in the case of a loved one, a warrior by trade, and a dedicated meat eater. Worst of all, Sunny's parents felt they had a divine mission to change Alex's life-style, to expand his consciousness. An evening with them was a guaranteed headache.

"Alex?"

"Yeah."

"Is it okay?"

"Yeah, sure," he said, padding slowly back into the bedroom. He knew the SOBs had a mission upcoming. A hairy one. He knew he could get in on it if he asked Barrabas or O'Toole. But if he went on the mission, he'd lose Sunny.

A buddy of his who had bought the farm in Iran,

Vince Biondi, used to call what the SOBs did "riding the ragged edge." The limit. That's why Nanos and the others stayed loyal to Nile Barrabas. Not for the money. Not because of any of the mystical bullshit that went around about him being "charmed," immune to alloys of lead. Barrabas spit and shit just like everybody else. But he took them to the ragged edge, the places nobody else would go, to do the things nobody else would do.

The appeal was to the ego. To pride. To the good old urge to self-destruct.

There was more to it, too.

There was a kind of unwritten code. You didn't turn your back on guys who'd covered your ass. On guys you could trust to always cover your ass.

It was the kind of thing Sunny would never understand.

She didn't like her ass covered.

"Alex?" she called from the shower.

Nanos struggled into his boxer shorts, then pulled on a pair of faded jeans.

"Alex, want to come in here with me?"

The Greek slipped on a sweat shirt with sleeves hacked off at the shoulders and stepped into a pair of battered jogging shoes.

"Alex, I've got something you like."

The short hairs rose on the back of his neck. But he didn't answer. Heaving a sigh, he turned and limped for the door.

7

J. Cruikshank regarded the decor of the Hotel Parima lounge-bar, the rotting fishnets, the cork-and-glass floats, the flashing red lights, with undisguised distaste.

Barrabas lit a cigar and regarded Cruikshank in the same manner. The California wheeler-dealer fell into a general category that the white-haired man had no use for: an overeducated, undertalented whiner. More specifically, he was a trader in secrets. As far as Barrabas was concerned, the only thing worse than a professional sneaky Pete was an unprofessional one.

Cruikshank was also as nervous as hell. When one of the Walletjes hash heads put some coins in the juke box and it gave forth abruptly with a heavy-metal selection, he jerked like a frog in a biology experiment. He was tall and thin, except for the doughy spare tire around his middle. He hid an angular pockmarked face under a full beard and mustache.

One of the Parima whores-in-residence accepted an invitation to dance and proceeded to snap pelvis with wild abandon, much to the amusement of the clientele.

"Why in hell did you pick this dump?" Cruikshank said.

"He has a thing for the down and dirty," Gunther Dykstra said. The blond giant helped himself to a cigar out of Barrabas's shirt pocket and lit it. "He has to come here because I won't let him use the Lido for his rendezvous anymore."

Gunther was referring to a rock nightclub he ran as a tax loss, a laundering operation for his smuggling profits and a revival showcase for sixties rock and roll, which he had a sentimental attachment to.

"Where is that Aeroflot guy?" Cruikshank said to no one in particular.

The "Aeroflot guy" was actually a GRU *rezident* in Amsterdam, ready and willing to finalize the deal with the newly formed international cartel of SOBs and Cruikshank.

"This has got to be him," Gunther said as a new customer entered.

A distinguished-looking man in a topcoat and suit slipped into the booth opposite Barrabas. "My name is Trutnev," he said. He pulled out some ID and showed it to them. "Can we talk in security here?"

"We're surrounded by the semisentient," Barrabas told him. "Nothing to worry about."

"You have the article?" Trutnev asked Cruikshank.

"It's still in the States. Safely hidden away. We are ready to move it as soon as we have satisfactory assurances from you."

"Yes?"

"Payment in full the moment the article leaves my hands in Rio," Cruikshank said.

Trutnev's face was expressionless. There were permanent dark circles under his eyes and a blue dark shadow of beard on his cheeks. "I understood that you would be coming along in person," he said. "You and your associates traveling to the location together."

"I have made other plans. My presence is not required at the location."

Trutnev clearly didn't like the sound of it. "This is not what we agreed upon before. There was to be official Aeroflot transport. And everyone was to travel together."

"Mr. Cruikshank has a chronic case of cold feet," Barrabas said.

"Also a touch of the yellow spine," Gunther added.

"It doesn't matter to us," the white-haired man went on, "whether he comes or not. My people are getting paid to deliver the article and install it. That's precisely what we intend to do."

Gunther gave Barrabas a nudge under the table. When he looked over at the doorway, he saw two men in car coats walking into the lounge-bar. Super cleans. Short hair. Freshly shaven. They slipped into a side booth, taking great pains not to look over at Barrabas and party. They had State Department written all over them. They were part of J. Cruikshank's surveillance entourage.

"I think it's time we broke up the festivities, gentlemen," Barrabas said. "We're drawing some unwanted attention from an official source."

"We will meet in Rio as planned," Trutnev said.

"Hotel Copa, Ipanema Beach," Cruikshank said. "Payment in full."

The GRU *rezident* nodded, then left the table and the bar.

The pair of State Department boys didn't get up to follow him. Instead, they ordered a couple of beers from the black bartender, feigning interest in the baby chimp the man had hanging on his arm. The monkey was part of the unique atmosphere—and aroma—of the club.

"I don't trust that commie bastard," Cruikshank said.

Barrabas clucked his tongue. "Here and I thought you were a man of strongly held political convictions...."

"Stuff it," the entrepreneur snapped. "I don't trust you either. Believe me, if I could've found anyone else to do the job on such short notice...."

"Great to know he has confidence in us," Gunther said.

"Whatever, we're stuck with each other for the

duration," Barrabas said. "Right now, I think it's time for you to take a walk."

Cruikshank rose from the table. "I'll be in place in three days. I'll expect you and your people in Rio when I arrive."

"Bye, bye," Barrabas said.

Cruikshank moved quickly out the door.

"Would you look at that!" Gunther exclaimed softly.

The State Department bloodhounds deserted their beers and scurried out the door in pursuit of the entrepreneur.

"Just like flies on shit," Barrabas said.

"My thoughts exactly." Gunther leaned back in the booth and puffed happily on his cigar. "Do you know something, I think your plan is actually going to work. I think the SOBs are going to get a red carpet all the way to the heart of Mother Russia."

Barrabas chewed his stogie. It did look pretty good, so far. The Russians were breaking their butts to transport the band of mercenaries exactly where they wanted to go. The bright side wasn't all that bright, however. Getting in was the easy part.

8

Anatoly Leonov dragged the scrub rag over the bare wood floor of the mess hall. He was trying to hurry, to get the job over with before one of the trusties came by to check the color of the water in his bucket. Such a check was certain to bring about an order to dump the oatmeal-colored fluid and start again with clean water. Drawing a fresh bucket from the camp well was one of the hardest things imaginable with broken ribs. The stabbing pain it brought on was unendurable. Worse even than the agony of scrubbing.

He actually thought he was going to make it, to finish before someone looked in on him, but his hopes were dashed when he heard footsteps behind him.

He shoved the rag back into the bucket and swished it around, not daring to look back. As he wrung out the rag, a pair of hands grabbed him by the hair and plunged his face and head into the filthy water. The top of his head rammed against the bottom of the bucket. As water rushed up in his nose, he panicked, struggling wildly. The powerful hands that held him down did not yield an inch. It dawned on him that he was about to be murdered. And there was nothing he could do to prevent it.

A noise, a bellow from above was audible even under water and through the sides of the bucket.

The hands let go of his hair and Leonov jerked his face up, sputtering, coughing.

"I said no one touches him," Kruzhkov growled at the back-stepping thief. "Whoever wins the bet, wins it fairly."

Leonov knew who was going to win the bet. And there would be nothing fair about it. Each of the bettors had chosen the day they thought Leonov would die. If he had not expired by natural causes before the day Kruzhkov had picked, the head bitch was sure to make himself a winner.

"If you're done," Kruzhkov told him, "go over and sit with the other goners. Take a rest."

Leonov tried to rise to his feet, but he could not. His back was too stiff. Like an aged animal he crawled on all fours between the rough tables of the mess tent.

Around the waning heat of the cook stove were gathered his new comrades, new brethren. The *dokhodyaga*. They lay sprawled like broken dolls, emaciated, coughing, their eyes round and unblinking. Leonov took his place among them. He closed his eyes and tried not to think about his empty belly, about his pain.

Someone nudged his arm. He looked up into

Kruzhkov's face. The bitch put something into his hand.

"Here, eat this," he said. "You've got to last a little longer."

Leonov clutched the small packet tightly, watching as his persecutor-benefactor walked away. Then he crawled off a distance from the rest to have a look at what he'd been given. He peeled back the oiled paper and saw that it was part of a chocolate bar. A prohibited substance in Slash One. For a moment he was possessed by the urge to wolf it down. He got it as far as his mouth before he caught himself.

I am no animal, he thought. No animal. He shattered the chocolate inside its wrapper, then crawled back to his fellow goners. Tenderly, one by one, he fed them all. Some did not respond even when the sweet taste was on their tongue; others seemed to brighten at once. He took the tiny bit he had saved for himself and let it dissolve in his mouth.

If he could have killed himself just to keep Kruzhkov from winning the bet, he would have. But Leonov was not a killer. He was a rational man in an irrational place. If chocolate would keep him alive for three more days, it would keep them all alive for two hours.

Leonov put his back to the heat of the stove. He was getting the chills again. His injury was serious. The ribs were shattered. On half rations his body could not fight infection.

He thought about his family, his wife and children, and prayed for their safety. He knew all too well that in the Soviet Union the sins of the father were also the sins of the son and the daughter. He had hoped to get them all out of the country before his last arrest, but it had been impossible. There had been many happy times before he had taken his stand, before the ostracism, the public humiliation, the prison terms, but somehow none of those times were as important as those that had taken place after. A family triumphs in times of trial. Suddenly he wanted more than anything to hold his son and daughter one more time. To touch their hair, their faces, to see their smiles.

The bout of chills became more powerful and he curled up into a ball on his side.

He opened his eyes and looked around him. Everyone near the stove was in the same fetal position. They were all going to the same place, by the same agonizing path.

He shut his eyes again and saw Valentin hanging in the tree, saw the hunk of his flesh roasting on the spit. A society that wastes such men is doomed, he told himself. As doomed as I am.

Perhaps Valentin hadn't suffered.

Perhaps.

If there was such a thing as a soul, and Leonov believed there was, he wondered what Valentin's had thought as it watched its mortal coil being consumed?

Some bitter joke, no doubt.

Something perfect for the occasion.

Dear God, Valentin, Leonov thought, how I need you now.

9

Barrabas stood on the vine-draped veranda of Casa Hatton and looked down at a gray, dripping world. The Spanish island of Majorca was Drizzle City. The *estancia*'s groves of fig and almond trees were leafless skeletons.

"They're all waiting for you inside," said a woman's voice behind him.

It was Dr. Leona Hatton, owner of the dilapidated rancho, the only female member of the elite mercenary force known as the Soldiers of Barrabas.

The white-haired man turned and looked at her. She was smiling at him. She had a soft beauty, warm, dark eyes, yet she wore her raven black hair cut radically short, like a man's. Barrabas often had the feeling that her father, General Hatton, had wanted a boy. What he had received was something much more special: a woman with spirit, physical strength and a keen intelligence. Dr. Lee was a combat surgeon par excellence; she also knew how to hurt as well as heal.

"I got it out of O'Toole," she said through her

grin. "This mission is for limited personnel. And you've got me on the list."

"Yeah, you're going," Barrabas told her. "You may not thank me for it later...."

"We'd better go in, now," she said. "The guys are getting anxious."

They entered the ancient house and walked down the hallway, stepping around the buckets set out to catch drops of water from the leaking roof. Dr. Lee and Claude Hayes had been working on the restoration of the place for almost a year, but there was only the two of them and it was a job for fifty.

When Barrabas entered the casa's main dining room, the assembled mercenaries stopped their joking and jiving. There were nine, counting Barrabas. Nine where there had once been thirteen. In the last twelve months they had lost four of their number. Chen, Boone, Biondi and Lopez.

"Gentlemen," he said, stepping up to a world map tacked to the wall. "You probably know by now that the job we're about to undertake will pay you each one million dollars. The highest salary we've earned to date. Since all of you except Chank Dayo have fought under my command before, you know that you'll earn every lousy dime of it before we're through. And in all likelihood some of us may not live to spend it. Maybe none of us will."

"This sounds like another 'nuke Iran' buildup," Nanos said.

"It's worse than the Iran mission," Barrabas told

them. "We're going to strike inside the Soviet Union. A thousand miles inside her western border."

Nobody said a word.

Suddenly a million bucks didn't sound like such a good deal after all.

"There's a dissident, a scientist, rotting away in a Siberian gulag." He pointed to a spot just east of the Urals. "Approximately here. It's our job to get him out alive. If any of you want to back out, do it now. Before I lay out the battle plan. I guarantee nobody will think the less of anyone who has better things to do."

"We got nothing better to do, Colonel," Billy Two said, "or we wouldn't be here."

"What's the plan?" Nanos asked.

"We will go in under the wing of GRU, at least in the beginning. Beck, maybe you'd better explain it."

The skinny computer genius rose from his chair. "We've got access to a high-tech processor board the Russians want for one of their biggest tank factories. We're going to use it as bait to get within striking distance of the gulag."

"You mean, we're actually going to give them the hardware to help them make tanks?" Hayes asked.

"What we're going to give them is a royal pain in the ass," Beck said. "A designed-by-Beck pain in the ass."

"I can only take five with me," Barrabas told

them. "And I've already made my choices. It's going to be O'Toole, Beck, Hatton, Billy Two and Dayo. Under Beck's instruction, we're going to install the processor board in their mainframe computer. That should take no more than a couple of days, tops. The gulag is roughly fifty kilometers from the factory. We aren't going to be able to do any surveillance of the target prior to the attack. GRU is going to be on us like a second skin. In order to hit the camp and get away clean we're going to have to liberate an aircraft. Obviously, we can only do that once. O'Toole, show them the satellite recon photos."

The red-haired man got up and stuck a pair of blowups on the map. "The camp complex is actually two prisons separated by a frozen bog. The larger of the two is for ordinary criminals and is the most heavily guarded. It also borders on the airstrip we'll have to use to get in and out. Our target is this smaller compound. It's double fenced. The inner barrier is made of wooden stakes, approximately twelve feet high. The outer barrier is wire. There are guard towers with machine guns and klieg lights. Also a kennel of guard dogs."

"How many are we going up against?" Billy Two asked.

"There's a forty-man force at the big camp. And twenty men at the smaller one. All of them are KGB and they aren't shy about dispensing lead. We do have a few things going for us, though...."

"Whew, that's a relief," the Indian said, grinning.

"First, these dumps were designed to keep unarmed people in, not to keep attacking forces out. Second, and this is even more in our favor, nobody has ever tried anything like it before. It's the last thing the Soviets would expect."

"Six against sixty doesn't sound like much fun to me," Nanos said. "Why not take more of us along to even up the odds, Colonel?"

"They're nervous about even six," Barrabas said. "It seems our reputations have preceded us."

This announcement brought forth a round of guffaws and a smattering of self-congratulatory applause.

"Don't worry, Nanos," Barrabas continued. "I've got plans for everybody on this one."

"How are we going to take and hold this airstrip?" Dayo asked.

"Firepower," O'Toole said.

"You can't bring firepower *into* Russia," Hayes said.

"That's right. We can't. All of our weapons will be supplied to us after we're inside," O'Toole said. "Some of you may have met 'The Fixer,' Walker Jessup."

"Good old Shamu," Nanos said.

"He's arranged for some Latvian free enterprisers to liberate everything we're going to need. It's all going to be Soviet stuff, of course."

"Killing commies with commie bullets," Billy Two mused. "There's a kind of justice in that."

"Okay," Dayo said, "I can see how we could isolate this prison pretty easily. I mean, it's way off in the boonies. It's the dead of winter. The roads are barely passable, if at all. The telephone lines could be cut, radio transmissions jammed or transmitters knocked out. But the problem is the distance from the camp to wherever the hell you expect to bail out. We're going to have a hundred MiGs up our ass before we get anywhere near a border."

"Billy Two tells me you're about the best bush pilot around," Barrabas said. "This is your chance to prove it. You're going to fly us to Finnish airspace."

Dayo seemed less than enthused at the prospect.

"Something wrong?"

The Eskimo started to say something, then abruptly changed his mind. "Nope, nothing's wrong. If anybody can get you out, I can."

"Where do the rest of us fit in?" Hayes asked.

"The transfer of the high-tech hardware is going to take place in nice, neutral Rio," O'Toole said. "You and Nanos are going to provide a little diversion so Gunther and Beck can get the goods out from under the noses of CIA and the State Department. You're going to have to disappear afterward." The Irishman paused and gave his colonel a questioning look.

"I'll tell 'em, Liam, if they haven't already

guessed," Barrabas said. "If we pull this one off, guys, we're *all* going to have to disappear for a while."

"GRU?" Nanos said.

The white-haired man nodded.

No further explanation was necessary.

"We can't train for this mission," O'Toole went on. "We don't have enough time, and in all honesty, it won't make any difference in the outcome. Either we take these guys by surprise or we take it in the shorts."

"I wish we were all going," Nanos said.

"You always land the soft jobs," Billy Two told him.

"I'll trade you."

"Go to hell."

"Billy, nobody's got it any easier than anybody else in this deal," O'Toole said. "It's either killing KGB or killing CIA. Anyway you look at it, it's a toss-up which is more hazardous to your health."

"Shooting our own guys?" Hayes said.

"If there's no other way to free up Gunther and Beck, you've got the green light," Barrabas told him.

"I hope this guy, this dissident, is worth it," Dayo said.

"Hey, explain things to the new guy, Billy," O'Toole said.

The Indian put his arm around Dayo's thick shoulders. "Chank, we're gonna stick it in Ivan's ear. The Wet Willy to end all. And everybody is gonna see it hanging there, all green and gooey. And they're gonna know we did it to 'em. The SOBs.''

"All of your passports, visas and plane tickets have been taken care of," Barrabas siad. "The Brazil contingent leaves tomorrow afternoon from Madrid. The rest of us will depart for Moscow two days later."

"That gives us plenty of time," Nanos said.

"Plenty of time for what?" Billy Two asked.

"To get on each other's nerves."

CLAUDE HAYES COULDN'T SLEEP. The drip of a roof leak in the bucket beside his cot in the rancho bunkhouse kept him awake. So did the idea of murdering a good guy to further a mission. He pulled on his rain poncho, got out a flashlight and headed up the gravel path to the casa, intending to heat up some coffee in the kitchen.

When he stepped up on the veranda he saw a light burning in Nate Beck's workshop, so he altered his course.

He rapped on the jamb of the open door.

The small, wiry man hunched over his workbench straightened up with a jerk. "Hey, Claude, come on in," he said. Beck was looking through a powerful magnifying glass on a stand, laboring over an intricate piece of microcircuitry.

"What are you making?"

Beck smirked. "Trouble. Big trouble. Do you know anything about processor boards?"

Hayes shrugged. "They use 'em for specialized functions, upgrades....:"

"Yeah, right. Well, this little beauty here is an exact duplicate of the high-tech hardware the Soviets have a hard-on for. It looks identical, works identical, but there is an important difference."

"Yeah?"

"This board has its own microcomputer. It's right here. I've changed the casing so it looks like an ordinary processor chip. The board will do what it's supposed to do, speed up performance on the IBM mainframe for twenty-four hours. After that, the microcomputer cranks up and knocks out the mainframe's central processor. I've programmed it to locate all ten ports and write over everything with zeros."

"Zeros?"

Beck nodded. "It's so cute, Claude. We go there to speed up tank production for them, and it looks like that's just what we've done...until we're safely on our way out of the country. Then this little number here starts erasing everything they have in memory. It'll take them a month just to figure out what's wrong. And then they'll have to reprogram the whole factory."

"Nate, you are a genius," Hayes said.

"Nope, the colonel's the genius. He told me what he needed and I just built it for him. We're going to substitute my board for the real one in Rio."

"Yeah, Rio," Hayes muttered, remembering what had him losing sleep.

"Is something wrong?"

"Yeah, something's wrong. I don't want to kill some American trying to do his goddamn duty," Hayes said. "That stinks to hell."

"If it was a clean job, we wouldn't have drawn it, you know that."

"Yeah, I know."

"So, look on the bright side. Maybe you won't have to fire a shot. Maybe we'll catch the sneaky Petes looking the other way."

"Thanks, Nate," Claude said.

He turned and headed for the kitchen and some coffee. He wasn't kidding Beck and Beck wasn't kidding him. They both knew their chances of lucking out were slim and none.

CHANK DAYO SAT with his back against the trunk of a fig tree, watching the sunrise, letting the cold rainwater trickle down his head and shoulders. A twig snapped behind him.

"Dayo, what the hell are you doing out in the rain?" Billy Two asked as he hunkered down beside him. "Have you been out here all night long?"

The Eskimo didn't answer.

"Trying to prove what a hard guy you are?"

Dayo looked up at his Nam buddy. They'd had a lot of good times together. Hairy times. Back in the Marines. They'd set records for having the most

Hueys shot out from under them, for having bedded the most bar girls in a single stint of R and R. If there was anybody he could tell his troubles to, it was Billy.

"I've been having this crazy dream," he said. "It happens almost every night. I dream I see myself blown away."

"A dream can't hurt ya."

"This isn't an ordinary dream. I've been having it for weeks. Before you and Hayes came and got me. It's got an airstrip in it. And there's shooting. And shouts, words I can't understand."

"Hell, it sounds like a dull weekend in Fairbanks to me," Billy said.

"I think it's a premonition. It's what's going to happen to me when we're a thousand miles deep into Russia. I'm going to buy a piece of that airstrip in Siberia and you guys are gonna be shafted, stuck with no pilot and the whole Soviet air force closing in for the kill."

Billy Two studied the Eskimo's smooth brown face. "This is what's been eating you, hasn't it? Christ! Here and I've been building you up to the others, telling 'em what a wild and crazy guy you are, and you make your grand entrance with your chin in your lap. Like your fucking bear died."

"I don't feel much like partying."

"Look, if you really believe you're going to buy it, why don't you tell the colonel you can't do it? He'll find somebody else to fly us out."

"I don't think you can get away from a true dream. I think it'll follow you and make itself come true no matter what you do or where you go."

"Hey, Chank, look, we'll cover each other," Billy Two said. "I'll make sure nothing happens to you. It'll be just like the old days. What do you say?"

"Sure, Billy."

"Why don't you come in and get some dry clothes on. Then we'll go up and get some breakfast at the casa."

"Right."

Billy Two watched his friend plod back to the bunkhouse. A true dream? Where in hell had Dayo dug up a load of bullshit like that? From paperback books, no doubt.

10

Claude Hayes peered over the edge of the nineteenth-story balcony of J. Cruikshank's hotel suite. The sand on Ipanema Beach below was snow white. What he could see of it. It was packed with Brazilians. Hayes thought about the Carioca girls he had seen earlier in the day, in their *tangas*, skimpy string bikinis. Lovely, lovely honey-brown ladies. He shifted the Mini-Uzi into his left hand, still admiring the view. The boardwalk that separated the beach from six lanes of traffic was decorated with a wavy, black and gray, asymmetrical design. A design meant to be viewed from the high-rise hotels that lined the beach. Directly below him was a café with white-and-blue umbrellas. Traffic on the coast road was bumper to bumper.

Everybody was checking out everybody else's equipment.

It was the perfect time for dirty business.

The black man turned and reentered the hotel suite. The big transaction was finally taking place. On one of the room's huge beds sat J. Cruikshank in swim trunks. His shoulders, back and spare tires were burned cherry red from an overdose of Rio sun. On the opposite bed sat the GRU man Trutnev. Each of them had an attaché case open on the coverlet. In Cruikshank's was the latest technology. In Trutnev's was the asking price: ten million dollars in cut diamonds.

"I am satisfied," Cruikshank said, putting down his jeweler's loop and dropping a handful of sample stones back into the Russian's case. "The processor board is yours."

Without further ado, they switched cases.

Trutnev viewed the object he had purchased critically. "If this device doesn't operate as advertised, I will be back for a refund."

"And you'll get it," Cruikshank snapped. "You know I always guarantee my product. And you know where to find me. Room 1910. I've no travel plans."

"Very well, it's time to go," Trutnev said, locking the case, then standing up.

Time to go.

Hayes felt a prickle of sweat break out on his forehead. He told himself that everything was going to be fine. He pulled on a thin cotton overcoat. The right front pocket had been slashed so he could stick his hand through and keep the Mini-Uzi under cover, yet ready to rip. All they had to do was walk seventy feet down the hall to the elevator. Gunther and Beck would be waiting inside. They would be carrying identical attaché cases. A switch would be made once the doors were closed, and Gunther and Beck would get out on the next floor and take the stairs to the street. Hayes, Nanos, and the three GRU men would remain on the elevator to the ground floor.

Once they reached the street, the State Department boys would home in on the Soviet with the case. And when they were stopped and searched, the case would contain business papers. Gunther and Beck would get clean away.

A piece of cake.

All five left the suite together. They were halfway down the corridor, with Nanos on point and Hayes bringing up the rear, when the trap was sprung.

Doors on opposite sides of the hallway opened simultaneously.

"Freeze!" shouted a clean-cut young man in a T-shirt and shorts. He had a .38 snub-nose in his hand.

There were lots more where he came from. All of them armed. All serious.

Hayes didn't even think about using his machine pistol. It was all over before it had begun. The advantage was to the boys from State.

It didn't stay that way. One of the GRU thugs was possessed of more balls than brains. Instead of surrendering to superior force and position, he opened fire through his overcoat.

Then everyone cut loose all at once.

Something creased Hayes's right ear. The shock numbed the whole side of his face. But not his trained response. He brought his Mini-Uzi up under the coat, trigger pinned, sweeping the kneeling men throat high.

"You dumb shits!" he shouted over the roar of autofire.

Out of the corner of his eye he saw the back of Trutnev's head bulge, then explode. Red and pink spattered the fabric-covered wall.

At the other end of the fracas, Nanos had much better cover than he did. There were two stocky GRU bodies between him and the muzzle-flashes. Bodies to suck up lead. The Greek knew all about the peculiarities of the 9mm parabellum round. He didn't try to shoot around the staggering Russians; he shot through them to hit the attackers.

The whole melee lasted less than twenty seconds. And when it was done, there were eleven newly made corpses on the corridor floor. And two men standing.

"Holy shit," Nanos groaned, sagging back against the elevator door.

Hayes looked at the Greek. He was misted from head to foot with gore. Hayes felt a sliding wetness against his neck. His shirt collar was drenched with blood. He touched his ear and discovered he no longer had a right earlobe.

"This was a setup," the Greek said.

"Yeah, I think so, too."

"J. Cruikshank was playing both ends against the middle," Nanos said. "Maybe we should kick the door in and take back the diamonds? Just for the inconvenience he's caused us."

"No time for that." Hayes bent down and freed the handle of the attaché case from Trutnev's death grip. As he pulled the case away, he shifted the inert body of a GRU man underneath. The guy's heart was still pumping. A jet of bright arterial blood spurted over the front of Hayes's overcoat. "Hell!" the black man snarled. "Dammit to hell! Hit the elevator button!"

Nanos did and the doors opened. Nate and Gunther stared out at the litter of bodies.

"Oh, fuck," Nate said quietly.

"There goes our neat little escape plan," Gunther said as Hayes shouldered into the elevator car.

Nanos followed. "From here on out we're just going to have to play it by ear," the Greek said. Then he looked at the side of Hayes's head. "Gee, I guess that puts you at a disadvantage, man."

"The plan stands," Hayes growled, jabbing the button for the next lower floor. He stripped out of his ruined topcoat and dumped a spent Uzi magazine, cracking in a fresh one.

Beck passed him a handkerchief. "Better put some pressure on that ear."

Hayes clamped the wadded-up cloth to the side of his head. "We've got no choice," he told the others. "We split up as agreed upon. Nanos and me will draw fire to buy you two time to get away.''

"Draw fire?" the Greek said. "I was thinking more on the order of taking cover in the nearest closet. The Feds don't like to see their boys down. And we really took 'em down."

"We're going out the front. Just like we planned. If we try to go out together, they'll get us all and the goods."

The elevator doors opened on an empty hallway. The exchange of attaché cases was made, then Gunther and Beck stepped out.

"Good luck," Gunther said.

"Don't give me that look, Dutchman," Hayes said. "You'd have done the same for us."

The elevator doors closed.

"How are we going to do this?" Nanos said. "The State Department guys are going to be looking for the GRU man, not us."

Hayes cracked back the bolt of his Mini-Uzi. "I think we can get their attention," he said.

"Bystanders, man. What about bystanders?"

"Aim high, run fast."

"Whoopee," Nanos muttered, watching as the illuminated numbers on the elevator floor indicator counted down.

On floor nine the car came to a sudden gut-wrenching stop. The doors parted to reveal a pair of elderly ladies in wide-brimmed straw sun hats leaning on each other for support. They started to enter the elevator automatically, but froze in their tracks when they saw the two occupants. Huge men, both blood splattered, armed and grinning up a storm.

"It's okay, girls," Hayes told them, jamming his thumb against the "door close" button. "Really. Nothing to worry about. Just take the next car." When the door shut, he told Nanos, "Get out of that frigging coat. You look like something out of a Mexican horror movie."

The body builder took off his gory topcoat and dropped it in a corner with Hayes's.

"We're gonna hit the lobby like the A-Team," the black man told him. "Lots of expended rounds, but no bull's-eyes. We go straight through the lobby, then across the street and merge with the beach crowd."

"Got it."

The elevator indicator flashed "L." Hayes didn't wait for the doors to come all the way open, but burst through the widening gap, nearly bowling over a young couple in swimsuits.

"Yeee-hahhh!" he growled as he charged, pointing his Mini-Uzi straight up, spraying the mirror-tiled ceiling of the Hotel Copa with a sustained volley of 9mm lead. As the old ladies upstairs had, the people in the lobby stood still, paralyzed at the sight of two big men running at them with blazing autoweapons. The ceiling crashed down around them, silver mirror bits shattering on the marble floor.

Everybody was screaming then. Hayes did his best imitation of a halfback, juking, weaving through the stationary people, heading for the glass doors.

The Feds were inside the lobby, guarding the exit from couches placed on either side of the doors. There were three of them, all in sports jackets and Lacostes, right hands jammed under their coats. They weren't scratching their armpits.

They won't shoot, Hayes told himself as he bore down on them. Not yet. As he whipped past their position, he saw the weapons come out from under the tropical-weight seersucker. Three Smith & Wessons trying to track him over the heads of the crowd.

"Move it!" Nanos shouted at his back.

Hayes hit the doors and kept right on going. He was halfway across the apron of white marble when the first shot sizzled past his left ear. Not two in one day, he thought, cutting hard right, jumping the low-shrub barrier and into the midst of the hotel's outdoor café. The white metal tables, huddled under gay blue-and-white sun umbrellas were packed with tourists. There wasn't much room between the tables. As Hayes ran on, a waiter straightened up at the wrong time and the two-hundred-pound black man slammed into him from behind, sending him across the table, into the food, headfirst into the lap of a very tanned grandmother.

"What in the world!" a young man at a nearby

table exclaimed, jumping up, trying to stop or slow down the running maniac.

He missed Hayes and caught Nanos. Or vice versa. The Greek gave the would-be hero a shoulder in the midsection that knocked him off his feet and set him down on his back three tables over. Umbrellas and tables crashed like dominoes.

The Mini-Uzi in Hayes's fist was six pounds of useless baggage. There was no way he could use it to defend himself on Ipanema Beach. He stuffed it muzzle-first into the nearest trash can. Nanos followed suit, dumping the attaché case, too.

They vaulted the shrub barrier in front of the café, shoulder to shoulder. From behind came the flat whack of pistol fire, and more slugs whizzed past them.

Ahead, the traffic on the six-lane divided street between the café and the beach was static. Bumper to bumper, cars, most of them expensive European luxury models, were all having their horns tested. Sun-browned rich boys hung out of open car windows, over the doors of convertibles, to gawk at the girls in *tangas* who paraded buns and breasts like Vegas chorus girls.

The two SOBs gave the boys something else to gawk at.

They ran right over the hood of a stopped Alfa-Romeo. Roughly four hundred pounds of raging bull trampled eighteen coats of hand-rubbed red lacquer and an eighth of an inch of precision-sculpted sheet steel. The shriek of the Alfa's hood was almost human as it buckled under their weight.

Hayes and Nanos jumped again, from the Alfa to a 350SL. German engineering fared no better than Italian.

"This is kind of fun," Nanos said as they leaped and landed in perfect unison on the hood of a British racing green Jag, putting a boulder-sized dent in it.

They jumped down and raced across the traffic islands. As they neared the final three lanes of traffic, Hayes began ripping his T-shirt off. "Time to go native!" he shouted to the Greek.

"What the hell," Nanos said, tearing his shirt off, too.

Then they played more "Frogger" for real on the hoods of expensive cars. As they hit the boardwalk, Hayes looked back. The Federal pursuit was just crossing the island. Hayes hopped on one foot, then the other as he stripped off his pants and shoes.

"Come on, Alex, let's go!" he said, dashing barefoot onto the sand and into the throng of slowly baking brown people.

Nanos dropped trousers, kicked off shoes and, clad only in his blazing red sport jock, sprinted after the rapidly disappearing black man.

After about a hundred yards Hayes slowed to a brisk walk, moving south, away from the hotel and the scene of the crime. To walk or not to walk wasn't his choice. The closer he got to the ocean,

the tighter the Brazilians were packed. There was so
little room between beach towels and sun chairs he
had to tiptoe in some places. Around him were at
least a hundred thousand people, all brown, all
nearly naked. Hayes looked over his shoulder.
There were no Feds in sight. No way could they find
them, now, not without the help of the Rio police,
the army and the National Guard.

Hayes waited for the muscular Greek to catch up.

"I didn't think we were going to make it out of
that café," Nanos confessed. "I have this unnatural
fear of dying with a bullet in my spine and a face
full of lobster newberg."

Hayes regarded Nanos's choice in beachwear. It
was worthy of a double take. "Hey, Alex, you're
friggin' bottomless!"

The Greek winced. A bevy of tawny, brown-eyed
Carioca girls were staring admiringly at his heavy-
duty glutes that the red jock strap did nothing to
conceal.

"Hello, there," Hayes said to them. "Wanna
snap his strap?"

"I vote that we keep on moving," Nanos said.

"No, wait a minute. I want to see if we still have
a problem with the Feds."

"I got the problem, Claude," Nanos told him.
"A Southern exposure. . . ."

"Why you cheeky bastard!"

"Hayes, cut the crap. And let me walk in front.
You can cover for me."

"And deprive these lovely ladies of a view of the eighth and ninth wonders of the world. Not likely. It's showtime, pal." With that, Hayes moved quickly to the waterline where he broke into a trot.

"Holy shit!" the Greek groaned as he ran to catch up.

His posterior was not only drawing appreciative stares and grins, but also catcalls and a smattering of enthusiastic applause.

NATE BECK thought he saw a Nazi every twenty feet.

He couldn't help it. It was his upbringing. In Beck's middle-class Jewish household, Rio meant only two things: carnival, and its attendant grotesqueries, and war criminals. For Beck, every Teutonic-looking male over the age of fifty was suspect. Accordingly, he gave I'd-dearly-love-to-rip-your-throat-out looks to stockbrokers, accountants, retail managers and civil servants.

"For Pete's sake, lighten up, Nate," Gunther said. "You're going to give yourself a brain hemorrhage in this humidity."

Beck looked up at the blond Dutch giant, at the please-be-nice smile on his great, sweaty mug. Gunther couldn't understand Beck's thirst for vengeance. He had no idea of its depth or the frustration that caused it. The Holocaust wasn't something Nate had merely seen in archival film on TV. In Hebrew school some of his classmates were the offspring of survivors; the stories they told gave him screaming, bolt-upright nightmares. And the implications of the Holocaust about the courage of the Jewish people, that they were meek, easily slaughtered, had always burned in his guts.

In an odd way it had all gelled with his movie-fantasy life. Although he was condemned to a small body, Nate Beck wasn't going to be meek when he grew up. He was going to be like Errol Flynn, John Wayne. An ass kicker for his people. Avenger of the wrongs of Auschwitz, Maidenek, Treblinka and the rest. In his boyhood daydreams, he, Errol and Big John came to South America to stalk and kill Nazis. To kill them like pigs in their beds.

Boyhood dreams have a funny way of turning sour.

Now that Beck was a trained, blooded soldier, the idea of killing war criminals had lost much of its appeal. What sort of justice was there in shooting crepe-necked octagenarians? The fact that he had lost his chance, that it was gone forever, infuriated him. If fighting with the SOBs had taught him anything, it was that true justice, more than anything, was a matter of timing.

He and Gunther had taken a cab from the Hotel Copa to the downtown section of Rio. Now they walked among the canyons of the tall buildings, the blowing trash, the smothering stink of diesel exhaust.

"Here it is," Gunther said, pointing at a small neon sign three doors down a narrow brick-paved alley. The pink sign said Le Club Harlan. Stairs led down to the basement-level bar.

It was dark and pungent inside. And it was cool. Before their eyes got used to the lack of light, a huge figure lumbered up to them.

"Where's the commie?" Walker Jessup asked in a soft drawl.

"Gone to commie heaven," Gunther said.

"The exchange got interrupted," Beck added.

"Yeah, so we saw," Jessup said, gesturing over his shoulder to the television set over the bar. On it was live minicamera coverage of the blood-soaked hallway. "How about Hayes and the Greek?"

"They made it to the lobby," Gunther said. "After that, we don't know. We couldn't stick around to find out."

"If they're in one piece, they'll turn up sooner or later," Jessup said. "Considering this is Rio, I'd bet on later. Look, I've got our Latvian over there in a booth. You've got the goods?"

Gunther and Beck held up matching attaché cases.

"Mine's the real one," Gunther said.

"Great, let me do the talking," the Texan said.

The three of them retreated to a corner booth where another blond giant waited. He was as tall as Gunther, but weighed fifty pounds less. His hair was decidedly MTV, crew cut on top and shoulder length on the sides and in back.

"Karlis, these are my associates," Jessup said as

they sat down. He took the case from Beck and placed it on the table. "And this is the final piece of merchandise to be moved."

Karlis opened the attaché case and looked inside. "So small," he said, grinning, "to be worth so much."

"Worth nothing to you if you don't deliver it," Jessup told him. "Nothing to our customers without Mr. Beck."

"Yes, you told me that...three times." The Latvian shut the case. "And it's a good thing our Mr. Beck is so important. Otherwise the temptation might be too great, despite your generous wages."

"You understand our requirements?" Jessup said.

"My friends in the pipeline will move this small thing and two large, sealed crates of test equipment to Riga as if they are Soviet contraband. After GRU and KGB have opened and searched the crates we are to repack them with a specified list of military items. AK-74s. Dragunovs. RPGs. Hand grenades. Then we will alter the weights of the crates on the official documents and air-ship everything to Ust Tavda."

"And our other requirements?"

"As far as any of my business partners know, this is a straight smuggling operation of high-tech hardware. The fix is in with KGB and GRU. They will receive their usual payoff for looking the other way...as is the case with all 'officially condoned' smuggling. The arms part of the deal will be handled by my brother and myself, and no one else will know about it.''

''I think that's everything.''

Karlis got up, case in hand.

''Remember, that has no value to the buyer without Mr. Beck,'' Jessup reminded him.

The blond man grinned and left.

''Bartender, *por favor*,'' Jessup said, ''three beers.'' He turned to Gunther and Beck and added, ''They've got good beer here. Cold-brewed, German style.''

Beck frowned. ''What's this standard payoff bit?''

''Part of the overhead. KGB-GRU knows about everything the Latvians do. They look the other way because the stuff smuggled in is usually harmless, usually consumer goods impossible to find in Russia, and because they get first pick. In this case it'll be a straight cash deal. In dollars, of course.''

''So the Russians are ripping themselves off?''

''No. KGB is ripping the Russians off. An entirely different kettle of fish.''

''Can we trust this Karlis guy?'' Gunther asked. ''He seemed kind of flaky to me.''

''I've done business with him and his brother before,'' Jessup said. ''They're okay. They like to exaggerate what they've done to hurt the Soviets. But that's the number-one sport of Latvian free enterprisers. Some of them will claim everything from sabotage of railways to the murder of policemen. Karlis and his people work on a more subtle level.''

"Yeah," Beck said, "AK-74s and RPGs. Real subtle."

"That's a special request. And very expensive. Their arms cache has been slowly, painstakingly accumulated...sometimes one screw at a time. It's like the Old West, a macho tradition, only hairier because to possess illegal weapons is to get your ass hung. I think the only reason they're willing to sell us their weapons is because KGB must have gotten wind of them. Time for a quick fire sale before they are caught with the goods and shut down forever."

"They should stick to the old standbys," Gunther said. "Much safer to smuggle in blue jeans and Susie Quatro records."

"Who is Susie Quatro?" Beck asked.

"I rest my case," Gunther said.

"Beck," Jessup said, "we've got to get you to the airport. Let's drink up."

The bartender deposited beer bottles and glasses on the table. The three men poured, then raised glasses in salute.

"To the mission," Jessup said.

They drank the cold brew.

"Nate, you're going to be an international celebrity once this is over," Gunther said. "The guy who tricked VPK, shut down a tank plant and helped rescue a famous defender of freedom. You'll get honorary degrees from Ivy League schools and have the girls crawling all over you.''

"Yeah," Jessup drawled. "Maybe the FBI will even take you off its Most Wanted List."

"Not funny," Beck said as the two big men laughed. "Not funny at all."

11

The walls of Major Grabischenko's office in the nine-story Khodinsk Building were windowless. It was a bunker inside of a fortress. Outside, thirty-foot walls and heavily armed guards with attack dogs patrolled in the snow. The internal security was so tight that no one in HQ staff could carry a briefcase into the building...or wear any form of metal. Plastic belt buckles were the approved style.

From this sterile environment, GRU ruled its considerable empire, which included a separate intelligence directorate in each of the Soviet Union's sixteen military districts and in each of the four Soviet fleets and four army groups deployed in Eastern Europe. It also included thirty thousand elite *spetsnaz* or "special designation" troops—Russia's answer to the U.S. Special Forces. The *spetsnaz* were trained in sabotage as well as terrorist methods.

One of the cream of the *spetsnaz* forces sat in a straight-back chair before Grabischenko's austere desk. The GRU deputy chief stared at Captain Balandin. A handsome man, he decided. But not too handsome. A touch of the Tartar in the slant of the eyebrows, in the wavy black hair. Captain Balandin's eyes were pale blue, intelligent, supremely confident.

"If, sir, as you suspect," Balandin said, "KGB has engineered, underwritten this whole project, put pressure on VPK to obtain the hardware through these particular mercenary agents, it is logical to assume that the foreigners' mission is to destroy or disrupt the Ust Tavda tank plant."

Grabischenko nodded. "That is something you will personally prevent."

"I assure you the mercenaries will be under armed *spetsnaz* guard the whole time they are here. They will not be allowed to mix with the population in Moscow. Their contact with the workers at the factory is necessary but will be limited and always under our supervision. I cannot promise these measures will make it impossible for them to disrupt the facility...one of them could throw his body into a machine on the assembly line. But short of that, short of suicide and a brief production delay, they will be unable to do us harm."

"I'm counting on you, Balandin," Grabischenko said. "The entire service is counting on you."

"I know, sir. I gladly accept the responsibility." The dark-haired man rose from his chair and delivered a crisp salute.

Grabischenko smiled at the captain's back as he left. There was no question about Balandin's first loyalty. About whether it belonged to the State, the Party or GRU.

Balandin was a good Communist, but he was an even better soldier.

12

The Aeroflot commercial flight from Zurich landed routinely at Moscow's Central Airport.

Barrabas peered out the breath-fogged window at the grim view. Huge banks of dirty snow were piled up alongside the runway and airport lights twinkled though it was only three in the afternoon. It looked cold and then some. Barrabas shuddered. He had been in Communist countries before. Been there with the intention of doing serious bodily harm to the indigenous pop. But this was different. This was the granddaddy of all commie rat traps. And the commie rats he was messing with were simply the best trained, the best equipped, the best motivated on the planet. The feeling of being closed in was something he had learned how to fight and therefore control. Any soldier working behind enemy lines had to get used to it. In this case it was a matter of scale.

Worst-case scenario, the white-haired man thought. Our Latvian contact fails to supply weapons adequate for rescue, and there is no way to acquire them. We would still wreck the tank plant. Still have our little bit of fun.

"Ever been here before, Colonel?" Billy Two asked.

Barrabas turned to the man sitting next to him in the three-to-a-row seats. "Only in my dreams."

"I hope we get to do some sightseeing," Lee Hatton said, through the gap in the seats. She, Beck and O'Toole were in the row behind the colonel, Billy Two and Dayo.

"Yeah," O'Toole said, "this is the last entry visa any of us is going to get out of these guys."

The plane taxied to a stop and the other passengers started to get up, gathering their coats out of the overhead compartments.

"Is somebody supposed to meet us?" Beck said.

"Our guides have been with us right along," Barrabas told him.

O'Toole got up and opened the overhead compartment. As he did, a stoutly built man in a blue blazer and hideous orange turtleneck stepped up to him.

"You will please remain in your seats," he said. "All of you."

Under the blazer, on the guide's right hip, there was a Makarov in a belt holster.

"No speak English," Liam said.

"O'Toole, don't mess around," Barrabas said.

"Right, Colonel." The red-haired man took his seat.

The SOBs watched as the plane emptied of passengers. Then the custodial crew came through and picked up papers, cans, bottles left behind. One of them was vacuuming the forward section when Lee pointed out her window and said, "Hey, look, we're getting the VIP treatment."

"Do they think we're trying to hijack this plane or what?" Beck asked.

Barrabas watched the BTR-60 armored personnel carriers circle and stop around the plane. There were lots of guns, heavy-caliber machine guns, small arms, lots of efficient-looking troops in snow gear. All the guns, all the soldiers, were facing their way.

"What were you saying about our reputation preceding us, Nile?" Lee said.

"Hey, a brass band would have sufficed," O'Toole told the blazer-wearing KGB man.

The plane's front door opened and a tall man in a parka with a fur-rimmed hood entered and walked quickly down the aisle toward them. As he approached he unzipped the parka, exposing a military jacket with a quart of fruit salad on the breast pocket.

"My name is Captain Balandin," he said. "For your own safety we have had the immediate area secured...."

O'Toole muttered something under his breath.

"If you will please put on your coats and gather up your hand luggage, we will escort you to your next stop."

The SOBs got into their own parkas and moved

into the aisle. Captain Balandin stepped out of the
way and let them pass. He fell into step behind Dr.
Hatton.

"May I help you with your bag?" he asked.

Lee gave him a small, polite smile and said,
"Thank you, no. It's not heavy."

Stepping out onto the plane's stairway was eerie.
It felt as though at the drop of a hat, a sneeze, all
those carefully aimed weapons would open fire and
grind them into so much hamburger.

Nothing happened, though. No hats dropped.
Nobody sneezed.

The ground was cold. Barrabas could feel it right
through the lug soles of his boots.

"Follow me, please," the captain said, waving
them toward a small bus painted dull olive. There
were metal bars across the side and rear windows.

"We should've gone first class, Chank," Billy
Two said to the Eskimo. "It never pays to econo-
mize."

Dayo took a seat in the drab bus and said nothing.

Billy sat beside him, determined not to give up
without a fight. "Mr. Gloom And Doom," he said
as the others were finding seats, "you should look
on the sunny side of things. It could be a hell of
a lot worse. In fact, it probably will be a hell of
a lot worse. It's almost dinnertime. If this is limousine service, imagine what their prime rib is
like."

Barrabas gave the Indian a shut-the-fuck-up look.

The bus started up and moved slowly away from the plane. In front of it, alongside it, behind it, moved the legion of armored vehicles.

"Say, Captain," Beck asked, "where are we going?"

"To Khodinsk Field."

"Not the *famous* Khodinsk Field!" Liam exclaimed.

Captain Balandin glared at the red-haired man. "Colonel Barrabas," he said, "if you and your people expect to be treated with respect, they should give us the same courtesy."

"He's right, O'Toole. No more warnings. Next time it comes out of your pay."

The bus and entourage crossed a couple of runways, then went through a chain-link gate. They finally stopped in front of a series of hangars. Beyond them was a thirty-foot-high wall and beyond it a tall, plain-looking office building.

"That's it, isn't it, Colonel," O'Toole said in a near whisper. "That's GRU headquarters."

Barrabas gave a slight nod.

"Please, everyone out and again follow me," Balandin said.

If Barrabas had any hopes of seeing the inside of one of the world's most secret complexes, they were dashed when he and his SOBs set foot outside the bus. Instead of walking toward the high, solid wall, the GRU captain led them toward an open airplane hangar.

The wind was really ripping. It cut right through protective layers of clothing.

"Colonel," Dayo said, giving him a nudge as they moved along, "that might be our plane, there."

It was an Ilyushin II-14, twin-engined, prop-driven airliner. The cargo doors were open and a heavily armed ground crew was loading a pair of bulky crates into the bay.

The SOBs walked a gauntlet of grim-faced soldiers into the hangar. Inside, more uniformed men stood at the door of a small frosted-glass-enclosed office.

Balandin took them over to the office, then said, "You understand that a strip search is a matter of protocol. We cannot allow you into our country, let alone a defense plant, without one."

Barrabas moved to the front of the line. "Take me first," he said.

In the small office, under the watchful gaze of five GRU officers and a staff doctor, Barrabas stripped down to his altogether. The concrete floor was freezing. He watched as they rummaged through his clothes, checking pockets, feeling coat linings, elastic waistbands. They did everything but run the stuff through a metal detector. It made the white-haired man want to smile. He might have, too, if it hadn't been so goddamn cold. He didn't need hidden knives, strands of wire, poison pills. Everything he required to take human life was at the ends of his arms and his legs. The only way they could really protect themselves would be to cut off his hands and feet.

When he saw the doctor pull on a rubber glove and stick his index finger in a jar of Vaseline, any slight urge he felt to grin thoroughly vanished.

"You will bend over," the doctor said, angling a desk lamp for the best illumination.

They checked his mouth, too. Every single tooth in his head. When they were done he was mad. There was nothing like a strip search conducted in subzero weather by a club-fisted service doctor to get the dander up.

He pulled his clothes back on and rejoined his people outside the office.

"How was it?" Beck said.

"You don't want to know."

"I'm going next," Dr. Lee said. "I'll be god-damned if I'm going to stand here and worry about it."

They watched her go into the office.

She was in there a long time. A lot longer than Barrabas.

"What the fuck!" O'Toole snarled under his breath. "What are those bastards trying to pull?"

It was on all their minds. A pretty woman stripped and forced to undergo a full body search by a group of soldiers. It was bound to be an extra-thorough examination.

"I say we give 'em two more minutes, Colonel," Billy Two said, "then we hand 'em their heads."

It was not the solution to the problem, as satisfying as the prospect sounded. Barrabas addressed the GRU captain. "If you don't have Dr. Hatton out here, front and center, in thirty seconds, me and my crew are going to board the next flight back to Zurich and you can stick your processor board straight up your ass."

Balandin wanted to give the white-haired man a hard time, but the threat made him back down. Without the SOBs to install the very expensive hardware, it was just so much junk.

When Lee stepped out of the little office she held her head high. The look in her eyes made Barrabas grind his teeth. They had hurt her. She was not in tears, but the hurt was there, the hurt and the anger. The team of examiners didn't know how lucky they were that this was the start of the mission rather than the end. Dr. Leona Hatton was a master at hand-to-hand combat. With a stick or a bare hand she worked with a surgeon's skill. She knew all the nerve points, the kill points, the break points. Only Liam O'Toole, out of all the SOBs, could stay in the ring with her for more than a minute or so. And O'Toole's staying power was more the result of his stubbornness, his ability to absorb punishment, than his ability to stand up to her. She was very quick, very smooth. There was no doubt in Barrabas's mind that Lee could have killed all five of her tormentors if given the green light.

She walked over to them and managed a grin. "Try and keep a tight sphincter, boys," she said. "I dare ya."

The strip search was entirely unnecessary. It was an excuse to exercise power and nothing more. However, it did serve another purpose, a purpose unintended by the GRU men. It united the SOBs in quiet, shared fury. When all the examinations had been completed and the Americans stood again together in the hangar, O'Toole said, "I hope these guys go with us to the plant."

"My thoughts, exactly," Billy Two said.

"We are ready to leave," Balandin told them. "Thank you for your cooperation."

They were led out of the hangar and over to the stairs beside the waiting Ilyushin. Behind them, about a dozen armed GRU soldiers followed.

"Quite an escort," Beck said, glancing back over his shoulder as he entered the plane.

"You ain't seen the half of it," Lee told him.

It was true. There were just as many soldiers already inside the plane. The odds were four to one in favor of GRU. And GRU was armed with AK-74s.

"Please," Balandin said, "you will each take a window seat. The flight will be two hours long."

Barrabas sat in the row behind Dr. Lee. He was not surprised when Balandin took a place right next to the woman doctor. Seriously ticked off, but not surprised. Like the other male SOBs, whether it was necessary or not, he felt highly protective of Dr. Hatton. It wasn't entirely because of her beauty. She was their savior should one of them catch a slug or a splinter of shrapnel.

Barrabas tried to listen in on their conversation, but he could not. They were speaking Russian.

13

"You don't mind if I sit here?" the Russian captain asked in his native tongue.

Lee Hatton answered in the same language. "It's your plane. Sit wherever you like."

"You speak Russian very well," he said, fastening his seat belt. "The dossier did not exaggerate."

The black-haired woman stared pointedly out the window at the gathering darkness. The Ilyushin's twin engines were heating up, making a dull whine as rpms climbed. She didn't like being hassled by strange men. Especially men like the captain who thought they were God's gift to women.

He persisted.

"I know much about you," he said. "Where you went to school, where you practiced medicine, your record of service to your country."

She ignored him. Her anger over the strip search had settled to a slow burn. She fanned the flames by purposefully recalling the details of her ordeal. The weakly smothered laughter of the GRU officers, their oaths of delight as they observed her violation.

She knew how to use her anger, how to focus it. The way the mission was turning out, with two dozen armed guards accompanying them, she was going to need every ounce she could muster. There was going to be a lot of killing before they reached Finnish airspace. If they reached Finnish airspace.

"What would your father, the general, think if he knew you were helping us build tanks?" Balandin said.

"Update your dossier; my father is dead."

"Yes, I know. But if he were alive, considering his long association with OSS, I would doubt that he would approve of what you're doing."

"My father and I didn't agree on everything," she said, glaring into his too-pale eyes. "It's called the generation gap."

"You do this for the money, then? Work with mercenaries and gutter criminals?"

"Yes, for the money."

Balandin smiled. "I don't understand. According to your dossier, you have a number of bank accounts in various countries. Your total deposits amount to almost half a million dollars."

"A girl can't have too much money."

"Or too much love."

Lee did not recoil when the captain put his hand on her knee. "Are you making an offer or a demand?" she asked flatly, staring him straight in the eyes.

"Whichever you prefer," he said, sliding his hand from knee to midthigh. His fingers dug into the flesh of her leg. "But I have found that a lot of women enjoy a demand. Even the ones who say they don't. The pleasure is in the struggle, the fear, the complete surrender."

Lee was being hurt, but she did not show it. His fingers were like steel clamps. "You have made these sort of demands on many women, I take it?" she asked evenly.

Balandin's pale-blue eyes twinkled. "Do you want to hear about my conquests? Would that excite you?" He did not wait for her answer, but continued eagerly. "The last was a blonde, willowy, pale. I saw her on the street and desired her, so I arrested her. She was seventeen. I took her in the back of a parked van I had commandeered for the interrogation. She fought once she realized what I was after. I had to break her jaw before she'd let me take her. What a bloody mess!"

Dr. Lee didn't need a further excuse to cause the captain intense pain. She put her hand on his, her fingertips reading it like a road map, the tendons, nerve centers. She applied pressure briefly, watching his face.

The agony registered in his eyes, in his slack jaw. He jerked his hand back and let out a soft whimper. What he wanted to do was to scream. He cradled his limp hand to his chest and shut his eyes tight, rocking forward and back.

"You asked which I preferred, an offer or a demand," she said. "From you I prefer neither. Try to keep that in mind."

14

If Barrabas couldn't understand the conversation going on in front of him, he could understand its abrupt end. He laughed softly to himself. If there was one knee on the planet not to grope, it belonged to Dr. Lee. The captain's attempted pass exposed a possible weakness in his character, a weakness they might be able to exploit later on. He hoped she hadn't hurt him too much. He laughed again. Some big, burly guys in uniform liked being kicked around the block by a domineering woman. If that was Captain Balandin's "thing," he was in luck. Leona Hatton, when pressed, could fulfill his wildest dreams.

The white-haired man settled back in his seat as the plane took off. He looked over the guards across the aisle from him. He'd never seen a *spetsnaz* trooper in the flesh before, but he was certain he was looking at some now. Hard, lean soldiers. Confident. Disciplined. He'd heard the stories about them. That no sleeping bags were issued to them even on winter maneuvers. The *spetsnaz* made do. According to official reports, there were two types of *spetsnaz* soldier: the raiders—*redoviki*—based in Eastern Europe, assigned to sabotage and assault behind NATO lines, and the huntsmen—*ikhotniki*—stationed in Siberia. There was also an anti-VIP brigade tasked with the assassination of enemy political leaders at the outbreak of war. This latter group was not uniformed and included Olympic-class athletes with freedom to travel in the West.

Barrabas's best guess was that they were being escorted by huntsmen, though their uniform was standard "air assault" without differentiating insignia.

The anxiety he had felt on landing in Moscow was gone now. It was the butterflies he always felt before the point of no return. The wondering if he had forgotten some key detail, the self-doubt that separated a great commander from a good one. It was too late for wondering. They were committed. And Barrabas could see the men they would be fighting. They were pros, but they were still only men. Men who could be made afraid, who could be killed.

In this case they would have to be killed. All of them. Somehow. Barrabas had no desire to be chased across the bleak winter landscape of Siberia by men trained to do just that.

THE PLANE BANKED SHALLOWLY and turned on its landing approach. Barrabas saw the town of Ust

Tavda. The town the T-72 built. It was lit up like a movie premiere. Spotlights pinned the twelve-story hostels, the sixteen-story apartment buildings, the twenty-five-story administration building and hotels. The residential areas were likewise lit up, as were the parks, still fountains and many town squares. Ust Tavda, a nothing Siberian hamlet, had grown up in a hurry, and it was damned proud of itself. The tank factory was just out of town, on a snowy plain, with plenty of room for expansion.

The Ilyushin touched down on the small airport runway, then rolled to a stop beside the two-story control tower. Balandin unbuckled his seat belt and stood up in the aisle.

"There will be a small delegation from the plant to greet you," he said to the SOBs. "It will be a short ceremony, then you will be escorted to your living quarters."

At the foot of the plane's ramp, braving a wind of fifteen knots with a chill factor of minus-twenty degrees, were the local dignitaries.

"Plee-azed to met you," said the town's mayor as he wrung Barrabas's hand.

The SOBs were introduced in turn to a short ruddy-faced man in a fur hat and coat, the plant director, one Ilya Shitov, and to Pyotr Vorobyev, the plant's chief engineer. The latter was quite tall, with longish dark hair and a heavy mustache. His English was excellent and it was clear he had braved the cold only to see Nate Beck.

"I am very anxious to see the processor unit in operation," he said. "If it does what we expect it to, we will increase production of the T-72 by a factor of 1.7."

"If there are no difficulties with the installation," Beck told him, "you should get your wish by tomorrow afternoon. I hope to be running test programs on the amended system by then."

"Wonderful!" Vorobyev said. "I want to tell you that I've long admired your work with computers. You were in the forefront of the revolution."

"Thanks," Beck said, stamping his feet to keep warm. "Maybe we'd better move along."

The tall Russian excused himself for his lack of consideration and waved Nate on toward the airport building.

After coffee and more glad hands under the watchful eye of armed huntsmen, Balandin announced that it was bedtime for the visitors.

The SOBs were herded toward a line of five identical, dark Lada sedans. They were ushered into Ladas three and four. The Ilyushin's three-man flight crew got into number two. The armed *spetsnaz* escort took the lead and tailing cars. The motorcade drove through the deserted but well-lit streets of Ust Tavda. It stopped in front of a twelve-story dorm building.

"This is it, huh?" O'Toole said after he had gotten out of the car. "Not too bad. I was figuring they'd put us up in the local jail."

The flight crew said good-night on the first floor, heading for their assigned quarters.

Even without them it was crowded in the elevator.

Six SOBs.

And fifteen guards.

And when they reached the dormitory room where they were to be housed it didn't get any less packed. The guards followed them right in and started picking out bunks for themselves.

"We're to be deprived of privacy for our own protection, I take it?" Barrabas said.

"You understand our security needs, of course," Balandin said. "Even though all the other occupants of the building have been temporarily relocated, we cannot allow you people freedom of movement."

"Why should we be treated any different than your ordinary, non-card-carrying Russian citizen?" Liam said.

"Pick out a bunk and hit it," Barrabas told his troops. "We've got a big day tomorrow."

As the others were unslinging their hand luggage and pulling off their coats, Barrabas addressed Dayo in a clear, matter-of-fact voice. "What did you think about that plane that brought us over from Moscow, Chank?" he said. "Ever seen one like it before?"

The Eskimo knew exactly what was being asked of him. "Only in picture books, Colonel," he answered. "And never with extended-range fuel tanks like that one had."

They had a problem.

And they all knew it now.

The only plane at the little airport was the Ilyushin. It was one thing for a trained, skilled pilot to jump into an aircraft he had never seen before and take it to the limit of its design capabilities. An aircraft with control markings in a language he could understand. It was an altogether different deal when the controls were marked in some unintelligible Cyrillic scrawl. And Dr. Lee would be of little help even though she was fluent in Russian. She wasn't a pilot and the terms, the names of the controls, often didn't translate easily. Not to mention the fact that they wouldn't have time to go over them. It was critical that they get off the ground ASAP.

Barrabas took the bunk below the Eskimo. He lay on his back and cradled his head in his hands.

"I wonder if the pilot speaks English?" he mused aloud. "If he does, it might be interesting for you to talk to him, Chank. You could swap horror stories."

"It's worth a try," Dayo said.

In a room full of the enemy, some of whom spoke English better than their American guests, Barrabas had neatly exposed a major flaw in their plan and had just as neatly given his people the only logical solution.

They were going to have to take the pilot along.

If he didn't speak English, Lee could do translation.

There was also another plus to taking him hostage. He could get the plane off the ground at Ust Tavda in a hurry and then Dayo would have time to get familiar with the controls on the flight to the gulag.

Barrabas closed his eyes.

Sleep was out of the question.

15

After a light breakfast in the dormitory dining hall, the SOBs were driven back under guard to the Ust Tavda airport to unpack their gear. The heavy crates had been moved into a hangar next to the Ilyushin II-14. They still bore intact inspection seals of KGB.

"All right," Barrabas said, "everybody grab a crowbar and get to it."

As the rest of the SOBs advanced on the sealed boxes, Beck hung back with the colonel for a moment. "We lucked out they didn't just move the crates to the tank plant and have us open them there," he said.

"Luck had nothing to do with it," Barrabas told him. "It was paranoia. Our captain wants to see for himself exactly what we're taking in there with us."

"It's what we're leaving behind that counts."

"Or so we hope."

With a splintering of pine, the shriek of nails being uprooted, the lids were pried off the crates. Inside were mountains of packing material, excelsior, cardboard batting. Barrabas and the others began lifting out the test equipment, devices that would measure the speed of the computer before and after the installation.

The white-haired man climbed into one of the crates to retrieve a dropped operations manual. As he did, he took a good look at the crate's bottom. It was false. There was a gap of more than two feet between it and the floor. Two feet that could contain enough weapons to flatten a gulag. Two feet that could contain nothing but air. They would have to wait to find out.

Barrabas rejoined his SOBs. They had the electronic gear all spread out on the hangar floor. It looked like the bargain table at a war-surplus store. "Well, Beck, how did it travel?" he asked.

The skinny guy shrugged. "It looks fine. But we won't know until we get it all hooked up."

Barrabas addressed the captain and two of his accompanying lieutenants who seemed as interested in the gear as Beck. "If it's all right with you, Captain, we're ready to load the equipment."

Balandin was satisfied that the gear represented no explosive threat to the tank plant. He waved for a waiting truck to back into the hangar.

"About the crates, Captain," Barrabas said, "we'll need them to repack for the trip home."

"They'll be safe here until then," Balandin told him. "Now, please, get back into the cars. My men will load the truck and deliver your equipment to the plant."

The SOBs piled into their Ladas and were chauffeured to the outskirts of town and the Ust Tavda tank factory. It was even more impressive from ground level. A truly enormous enterprise. Its main building was over two klicks long and half a klick wide.

And its vast parking lot was full of snow-covered tanks.

Shitov, the plant director, met them at the front gate and with Balandin acting as translator, took them on a brief, closely supervised tour of the premises. The plant was a city unto itself. It had its own railroad that moved the tank carriages along the automated assembly lines. The area covered was so broad that the tour had to be conducted from a fleet of motorized golf carts. The SOBs rode three to a cart with a worker doing the driving. The *spetsnaz* guards drove their own.

The din of the heavy machinery, the roar of 780-horsepower diesel-tank engines being tested, provided Barrabas with the cover he needed to get some important work done.

He leaned against the doctor who sat next to him. "Lee?" he said right in her ear.

She looked at him with those big, soft eyes of hers.

And for a moment he couldn't ask it of her. Not because he thought she wouldn't do it. Because in his guts he didn't want her to. What he wanted and what the mission demanded were two different things.

"I think you were a little rough on the captain yesterday," he said.

Her eyes narrowed.

"We could use his cooperation tonight," Barrabas told her.

"Tonight?"

He nodded. "We're set. No reason to wait."

"Cooperation is something the captain wants from me."

"All that's required is getting his attention focused elsewhere at a critical moment."

"That will be no problem," she said, turning to face front again. A smile lit up her pretty face. "Speaking of attention focused elsewhere, would you look at Starfoot."

Billy Two rode in the other golf cart. He was sitting right up front with the driver, who happened to be female and built in stereotypical Russian fashion, not unlike one of the tanks that had made Ust Tavda famous. Out of view of the plant director and the GRU captain, and the entourage of *spetsnaz* guards, the Indian passed his hand around the stocky woman's back, under her padded jacket and over her left breast.

"What's got into him?" Barrabas said.

"The lure of the different?" Lee suggested. "You know, foreign cultures, strange customs. . . ."

"There's nothing different about it," Beck told them from the cart's front seat. "He was born horny."

BILLY TWO GOT THE ITCH the moment he climbed into the golf cart. It was odd because before he sat down next to the driver, sex was the furthest thing from his mind. His thoughts had all been on survival. There was something about the woman driver that put other ideas in his head. A kind of availability she radiated like cheap perfume. She wasn't by any means the worst-looking female he'd ever chased, either. Her face was plump but not flabby, and there was a serenity to it. Her eyes were blue, and the wisps of hair he could see sticking out of her watch cap were flaxen. Stout, hell, yes, she was stout. He preferred to think of it as well upholstered.

"Do you speak English?" he had whispered to her during a lengthy tour stop.

"A leetle."

"My name's Billy."

"I am Sasha," she said, giving him a look that translated the same way in all languages. Hot.

Maybe it was the inappropriateness of the act, the danger of being caught, but he couldn't keep his hands off her body. And the more he touched, the more he wanted to touch.

While the GRU captain droned on, dutifully rendering the plant director's boring and exaggerated production statistics into English, Billy Two was working his big mitt under her clothes, to her bare skin.

It was soft and warm.

She looked straight ahead, nodding at the proper moments in her employer's speech, pretending that the huge Indian wasn't caressing her, making no move to push his hand away.

Billy felt the wide elastic back strap of her industrial-strength brassiere, then explored further, following it to the hollow of her armpit and from there curving around her sturdy rib cage to a truly Wagnerian breast.

Her hand dropped from the steering tiller to his knee.

Billy tried to undo the grappling hooks that held the bra's back strap together. He was still trying when the tour came to an end and the quintet of golf carts parked in front of the plant's computer center.

"I want to see you," he told the driver. "Do you understand?"

She nodded. There were roses in her round cheeks. Not from the cold in the unheated plant, but from the passion pounding in her veins.

"Come to the dormitory. 11:00 P.M. I'll watch for you."

He got off the cart and joined the others on their way into the computer center. Inside the protected enclosure the air was stuffy, overheated, but the din of the plant was gone.

Chief-engineer Vorobyev ignored everyone but Beck. Like a high-school sophomore on his first heavy date, he steered the skinny guy around the room, pointing out features of interest.

Beck's attention was riveted on the IBM mainframe that dominated the center's floor space. From it snaked thick cables that connected every inch of the tank plant. Attached to it were video-display terminals and closed-circuit TV monitors that kept tabs on every movement of the assembly line.

While Nate was involved with the chief engineer, Liam took the opportunity to sidle up alongside Billy Two. "Like 'em hefty, huh?" he said.

The six-foot-six-inch Indian looked down on the stocky red-haired man. "I'm no snob when it comes to women."

"No slouch, either," O'Toole said. "That was some fast work. Real professional. To tell you the truth, up until now I never believed all those stories you and the Greek tell about working as full-time gigolos in Florida."

Billy Two grinned.

Liam got that wicked look in his eyes. "And it's only right that a couple of pros go head to head."

Billy's grin faded. "Say what?"

"In case you hadn't noticed, your new girlfriend is a KGB agent."

NATE BECK SUPERVISED the placement of the test equipment as the *spetsnaz* men brought it in. When the last of it was moved into the computer center, Vorobyev stepped up to him.

"If you are ready," the chief engineer said, "I

will shut down the plant, and you may begin the installation.''

Beck nodded.

Vorobyev barked a series of commands at his underlings who set about putting the giant to sleep.

In a way Nate felt sorry for the chief engineer. The guy was like a kid with a new toy. Eager to experiment, to learn, to know. The problem was, Vorobyev's pride and joy, the Ust Tavda plant, manufactured instruments of death and oppression. If the chief engineer could think of T-72s as mathematical units, as abstracts, Nate Beck could not.

Even though Beck felt sorry for Vorobyev, he was proud of his own accomplishment, the neatness of it, the purity of all those zeros wiping out the stored memory, that compendium of tedious man-hours spent in accumulating trial-and-error data. Sure the Soviets had a backup memory system. It was just as sure they wouldn't dare use it until they were certain they had the problem nailed down.

Therein was the rub.

Beck had designed the new processor board so it would pass every conceivable test. And if they found it was the cause of the problem, if they located the camouflaged micro-computer, they still would have to put the enormous system back together again. If they could. Large computer systems were touchy things.

He took his tool kit from the desk where the others had set it, opened it up and set up shop. He whistled as he unscrewed the back panel of the main-frame.

Dayo came over and helped him with the job.

In five minutes they had the entire back of the unit open to view.

"Marvelous piece of work," Beck said appreciatively.

He opened the attaché case and took out the processor board.

Vorobyev was right there, peering over his shoulder. "Here, hold this for a minute," he told the chief engineer, handing him ten-million-dollars' worth of technology. "And don't drop it."

The little joke went right over Vorobyev's head.

Beck studied the field engineering manual he had brought along, then took back the processor board. Deftly he removed the existing board and inserted the new one.

"There you go," he told the chief engineer.

Balandin was less than impressed. "For this we had to bring six people here?"

"I had to have somebody to mop my brow, didn't I?"

"Don't worry, Captain," Vorobyev said, his face flushed with an excess of scientific zeal, "the real trick comes now, in the testing."

"That's right," Beck said, "the real trick comes now."

16

"You realize that your hot date is with the KGB," Barrabas said softly to the Indian.

Billy Two turned away from the dormitory window where he was eagle-eyeing the nighttime street below. "Afraid she's going to pump me for information, Colonel?"

"Among other things."

Billy Two grinned. "Everything's gonna work out fine. I can't think of a better excuse to lure a couple of our GRU buddies outside. As far as love goes, I'll take it anywhere, any way I find it. Even in Ust Tavda with a Party member. Afterward I'll take out my escort."

"Do it quietly," Barrabas said, glancing back at the tiers of occupied bunks. About a third of the guard force were playing cards. The rest were asleep or nearly so.

Billy Two stepped up to where the captain lay on his bunk. He bent down and said, "Excuse me, sir, but I'd like to go outside for some air. Could you detail a couple of men to go with me? For my own protection, of course."

Balandin scowled at him.

"In the interest of international goodwill and a speedy completion of the task at hand?"

The Indian had struck nerve. Balandin growled an order to the men playing cards. A pair of them stood up and started pulling on their coats and gear.

"Thank you, sir," Billy Two said.

As the Indian headed for the door, O'Toole yanked the case off his pillow and threw it at him. Billy one-handed it. "What am I supposed to do with this?" he said.

"Yeah, you're right," Liam said, ravaging another pillow for its case. That, too, he threw at the Indian. "She's definitely a two-bagger."

"O'Toole, you've got no class."

"I hear that a lot."

Billy chucked the cases back at him and, with his escort of *spetsnaz* huntsmen, exited the dorm barracks and made for the elevator.

"You guys speak English?" he asked as the doors closed and the car started down.

The taller of the two crew-cut men answered. "Of course. Also French, German, Spanish and Arabic."

"I got a honey waitin' for me outside. How 'bout giving me some slack?"

The huntsmen gave each other doubtful looks.

"A woman. Waits for me. Outside," Billy Two said. Then he made a universal hand gesture. A ring of thumb and forefinger of his left hand and the index finger of his right hand pistoning in and out.

The grim-faced *spetsnaz* warriors grunted their assent.

Not even a smirk, Billy Two thought. It was a set-up, all right. Everything agreed upon beforehand. Well, the goddamn KGB was going to get more than it had bargained for.

Outside the dorm building the air temperature was in the low teens. Not counting the chill factor. Billy Two had no performance anxiety. He was used to roughing it.

Sasha walked right up to him. She was so bundled up in coat, muffler and wool cap she might have been either sex. Or no sex. He put his arm around her shoulders and pulled her close. Her eyes were bright, and her nose was red and slightly runny.

That didn't stop him from planting a great hot and hungry kiss on her mouth. When he drew back, he turned to the escorts and said, "The lady and I are going to wander over behind that bush for a while. Okay?"

The huntsmen pointedly turned their backs to him.

Maybe *spetsnaz* don't do it, Billy Two thought as he steered Sasha to the limited seclusion of the nearby snow-covered bushes. Or maybe they only do it to each other?

Sasha knew exactly how to handle the situation outdoors on a frigid winter night.

Quick.

And with gusto.

There were so many layers of clothes between their bodies it was difficult for Billy Two to throw himself passionately into the fray. He would have dropped his pants, instead of merely unzipping his fly, but he was afraid of getting frostbite where it would be difficult to explain. Any difficulty he had in building to a peak was a sheer delight for Sasha who peaked and repeaked and peaked again. By the time the crucial moment came for him, his KGB lover was shrieking like a madwoman. He redoubled his efforts, throwing all of his weight into the thrusts and succeeded in pile-driving her across the snow, moving her in roughly ten-inch increments.

All thoughts of interrogation, of duty to motherland, gone, Sasha locked her short legs around Billy's lean waist and clung for dear life.

Billy thought they trained KGB women ops in sex-control techniques. They weren't supposed to lose it in the middle of the fray. Sasha was losing it and then some. She had his lower lip clenched between her teeth and was biting down hard. Her lower extremities were rolling like thunder.

When, finally, her thrashing under him ceased, he nuzzled her ear with his nose. "So, how do you rate the old red man wham-bam?" he said.

Her answer was in a foreign tongue. Her tongue. Thrust deep in his ear.

The problem with a down-and-dirty snow hump is the knees. They always melt the snow and end up wet from midthigh to shin. As Billy straightened up and zipped up, the arctic wind hit the wet material. He shivered and did a little foot-stamping dance.

"Hey, I've got to run," he told the KGB woman. He gestured back at the *spetsnaz* troopers waiting impatiently by the front entrance of the dorm building. "I sincerely appreciate the hospitality. You've just made a friend for Mother Russia."

"Tomorrow we talk," Sasha said, giving him a hug. Then she turned and walked away. The whole back of her body, from woolen cap to coat to boots was white from ground-in snow.

The huntsmen regarded Billy with disgust as he returned to the building's front. He greeted them with a broad smile. "You're next," he said.

The taller of the two frowned. "You said what?"

"Oversexed," Billy lied. "Your Russian ladies are oversexed. And underloved. You should play with them instead of your AKs."

The huntsmen were not amused. "Come," the tall one said. "We go back, now. You have had your fun."

No, Billy Two thought as he climbed the building's stairs with escorts in tow, the fun is just beginning.

LEE PUT HER HAND on Captain Balandin's shoulder and gave it a gentle squeeze. "Is there someplace private we can have a talk?" she asked.

The GRU man eyed her suspiciously. "For what reason?" he said.

"Even in Russia, a woman can change her mind, can't she?"

The captain brightened visibly. He took her hand from his shoulder and turned it palm up, planting a kiss in its soft center.

Lee repressed a shudder of loathing. "Not here, please," she told him. "Not in front of the others."

The captain rose from his bunk. He clamped a proprietary arm around her slender waist, making sure the SOBs and his troopers saw exactly what was transpiring.

As far as Lee was concerned, that was just fine. It would only make it easier for her to do what she had to do. Balandin would think twice about calling for help when his men knew he was up against a "mere" woman.

"There is a room we can use at the end of the hall," he said, steering her out of the barracks. As he did so, his hand at her waist dropped to cup her bottom. "I'm glad you had a change of heart," he told her, giving her a hard, stinging smack with the flat of his hand.

Lee wanted to wipe the smug grin off his face. She did not. The end of the hall loomed nearer. Balandin's just deserts were only a moment away.

He opened the door to the small dark room and turned on the single bare light bulb. It was a custodian's closet. Along one wall were shelves with various bottles and metal containers. Opposite were the usual complement of mops, buckets, brooms and plumber's helpers.

"How romantic," Lee said.

The captain grabbed her by the arm and shoved her in. Lee did not struggle, but permitted him to close the door behind them. She faced him without fear, though he easily outweighed her by a hundred pounds.

"You hurt me in the plane," he said, his eyes gleaming with anger and lust. He swung on her with blinding speed.

Her head snapped to the right; white light exploded inside her skull, disintegrating into thousands of tiny falling stars. Then blood surged to the site of the blow; half her face was on fire.

"Now I'm going to hurt you," Balandin said, reaching out for her throat.

His hand closed on nothing.

Lee ducked under his lunge and stepped around him. As she did so, she drove an elbow hard into his right kidney. It was a solid blow, aimed as only an expert in human physiology could aim.

Balandin made a soft sound, an expulsion of breath, his whole body tensing as the pain shot up and down his side. His paralysis was momentary, but it lasted long enough for Lee to get into position behind him. She pivoted to the inside and punched, throwing every ounce of her 120 pounds into the blow. A blow placed in exactly the same spot as the first.

The results were dramatically different.

Because of the power.

Because it was blow on blow.

Balandin said "Whhuhh" and dropped to his knees as if all his strings had been cut. He gasped for breath, fighting against the agony that convulsed his rib cage.

Lee grabbed him by the hair, bent his head way back and delivered a precise rabbit chop to his voice box. It was not enough to crush the windpipe, but it was enough to render him momentarily mute.

She let go of his hair. "This isn't for me," she told him. "I'm not a freak like you. I do believe in simple justice. This is for all the other ladies you've hurt." Lee snap-kicked him high in the back, sending him crashing headfirst into the back wall. "Get up!" she snarled.

The GRU man dragged himself to his feet. He turned and opened his mouth to yell something at her, but only a hoarse croaking sound came out.

"Speechless, huh?" she said.

Balandin jerked his stiletto free of its belt sheath. He didn't want to beat her with stealth or tricks; he wanted to do it with animal threat, to terrify and pound her into submission, to rape her and stab her to death. Before he lunged at her, he undid his fly and showed her what else he had in store. He was definitely ready to rape.

Then he charged.

What followed happened so quickly he never even saw it.

Lee was completely relaxed, so relaxed that she soberly considered her choices in the matter. Knife hand, claw hand. Or "monkey grabbing the peach." She made her mind up in a nanosecond, thrusting knife hand, palm up, fingers stiff, deep into his exposed crotch, then snapping claw hand out.

It did not come back empty.

Balandin fell to his knees, eyes wide with shock as he saw his testicles there in her fist, no longer part of him. Then the pain hit, and he collapsed to his ashen face on the closet floor.

Lee slipped the vile handful into one of his side pockets, then pulled an empty coat hanger down from a rack. She untwisted the hanger and retwined it around Balandin's wrists. Then did the same to his ankles. She took three more hangers and the captain's knife.

As she stepped over him and reached for the doorknob, he let out a weak moan. She could not resist a parting shot.

"Stay hard, guy," she said.

BILLY TWO ENTERED THE ELEVATOR ahead of the huntsmen. He put his broad back to the wall and watched as the tall one pressed the floor button for the dorm. The other trooper was watching him, arms, shoulders relaxed, feet planted. These two had drawn this kind of duty before. If there was no way to take them both by surprise, he would take what he could get.

As the car started up with a jerk, Billy Two kicked. Hard and straight, right at the solar plexus of the shorter huntsman. The guy reacted with incredible speed, turning the blow away with the edge of his left hand. The shock rippled up the Indian's leg from ankle to hip. He went with the momentum of the block, all six and a half feet of him spinning to deliver a wicked back kick to his enemy's chin. Heel to chin. The jarring impact registered in the shudder in the man's thick neck, in the sudden emptiness in his gaze.

Something hit Billy from behind, right at the base of his skull. His own knees buckled as blackness filled his head. Billy fought back the darkness and turned, crouching.

"No more games," the tall man said. His hand dropped to the butt of his still-holstered Makarov.

Billy had no choice but to play games. The colonel and SOBs were depending on him. He knew the guy was going to draw, so he kicked for the gun hand, the top of the wrist, as the autopistol cleared leather. The ball of his foot clad in a size-fourteen boot shattered the wrist, smashing it against the steel-sheathed wall of the elevator car. The Makarov clattered to the floor.

Howling with pain, the tall huntsman threw a

roundhouse left that grazed Billy's cheek. The Indian countered with a forearm across the man's unprotected throat, hurling his opponent to the wall, pinning him there.

There was a rustle of movement behind him.

Billy reacted. He grabbed the tall man's coat front, turning him as a shield.

The stiletto passed through a bit of Billy's parka and continued on, deep into the side of the huntsman. For an instant the three of them were almost nose to nose, chests, elbows, legs touching. Then there were only two. The double-edged blade had nicked some major artery. The tall man slumped away from Billy's grasp, his body twitching frantically as synapses shut down and nerves fired, then misfired for the last time.

The other huntsman twisted his blade free and drove it at Billy's guts. The Indian caught the hand about to kill him by the wrist. The trooper was strong and determined. Billy could not turn the point aside and his attacker could not drive the bloody blade home. They stood locked like that, bodies trembling from the strain as the elevator climbed.

Billy tried to shift his man off balance, feinting one way, moving another, but the huntsman either anticipated or recovered before any advantage could be gained. All that Billy accomplished was to turn the man's back to the elevator doors.

He glanced up at the floor indicator. They were

almost at their destination. He redoubled his efforts, throwing his whole weight forward, trying to get operating room. The smaller man gave up ground grudgingly. He, too, knew they were near the barracks floor and reinforcements.

As the elevator slowed, a glint of excitement lit up the huntsman's otherwise impassive face. He bared his teeth at Billy Two, opening his mouth to call for help as the doors behind him slid apart.

Over the trooper's head, Billy saw Lee Hatton. She stood at the entrance to the elevator. He did not have to explain the situation to her. She read instinctively the danger they were all in.

The pretty dark-haired woman reacted at once. She dropped a loop of untwisted coat hanger down over the man's head, over the point of his chin. Grunting from the effort, she cinched the garrote tight, making the black wire slice deep into the muscle and tendon of the huntsman's neck.

Whatever words of warning the *spetsnaz* fighter was about to utter were forever lost. His voice, his air, the blood supply to his brain were cut off.

Lee locked the wire noose in place, twisting the free ends of the wire, hand over hand.

The trooper dropped his knife, clawing at his own throat. It was a battle that could not be won. His face purple, his tongue poking out huge and blackened between bloated lips, he collapsed against the Indian.

"Thanks, Doc," Billy Two said, letting the corpse drop to the floor of the car.

Lee picked up the Makarov from a corner. She jacked a live round under the firing pin. "Let's get this show on the road," she said.

17

The *spetsnaz* playing cards looked up from their game when Lee returned to the barracks. That she was alone didn't alarm them. They were too busy being amused at the thought of what their captain had done to her.

Lee moved between the tiers of bunks to where Barrabas lay.

"So?" the white-haired man said softly.

"Three down and twelve to go."

She sat on the edge of the bunk beside him. Barrabas put a consoling and concealing arm around her shoulders. She took the two captured Makarovs, a knife and a pair of untwisted coat hangers from inside her shirt and put it all on the bed between them.

Barrabas chose one of the coat hangers for himself, then got up from the bunk. His broad back blocking the view of the cardplayers, he handed Dayo, who was in the upper bunk, a pistol. Lee likewise passed Nate, in the lower bunk opposite, a gun, and O'Toole, in the upper, a knife.

The white-haired man kept his right hand behind

his back as he sauntered over to the card game. The *spetsnaz* paid him no mind. Barrabas looked over the shoulders of each player in turn, apparently checking out the hand each man had drawn but actually working himself into position on the far side of the table.

"Come over here, Lee," he said. "Take a look at this."

Dr. Hatton complied. She stood behind the seated man on Barrabas's right.

"Ahh-choo!" Barrabas said, covering his nose and mouth with his empty hand.

"Bless you," said one of the huntsmen.

"Bless you, too," Barrabas said, swinging the wire loop over the man's head, twisting it tight.

A split second later, Lee was doing the same thing to the trooper next to him. The other *spetsnaz* were momentarily dumbfounded to see their compatriots gagging, turning a grotesque beet red from the neck up. But only momentarily.

As two pairs of huntsmen's heels thudded convulsively on the floor, the rest of the card game broke up. Troopers jumped to their feet.

Liam, from a kneeling position on his upper bunk, threw the knife with deadly accuracy. It pierced the throat of a man facing him, penetrating clear to the metal hilt. The huntsman grimaced in agony, lips peeling back. Blood sprayed from between his clenched teeth as he fought to pull the blade free, as he toppled forward onto his face.

Another blade handle appeared to suddenly spring from the back of the trooper nearest the door. The razor point drove in below his right shoulder blade, skewering his heart. Billy Two ran into the room, shoved the dying man across the table, grabbed the knife handle and twisted it out.

Nate Beck was up and moving, too, charging the two men who still stood. He had the commie auto-pistol in his right hand and the pillow from his bunk in the other. He rammed the pillow into the closest man's back, then the muzzle of the Walther-style automatic into the pillow.

He fired twice. The pillow muffled the hard reports, but the 9mm slugs went through the huntsman's torso.

On the tiers of bunks, the rest of the guard force was coming around, waking up, realizing that something was happening.

Chank Dayo moved among them, pillow in one hand and Makarov in the other. Some were tangled in their bedcovers, some were on their feet, jumping for their weapons. It was not a fair fight by any means. Chank jammed a pillow against a head and fired. He pulled away, feathers floating in clouds of cordite smoke and brains and blood splattering across the floor. He pressed the pillow against a chest and fired. He saw the grimace of pain and the shock of bullet entry and exit register on the trooper's face. He saw the slug spark off a metal bed frame as it continued on.

It was execution, not war.

But it had to be done.

Nate shot the last cardplayer through the heart as the other SOBs ran among the bunks.

O'Toole had caught a man from behind as the trooper tried to roll from his bunk. The power in the Irishman's forearms and wrists was more than a match for the *spetsnaz* neck. He snapped it with a quick twist and let the jerking corpse fall away, moving on, looking for a fresh target.

There was an odd kind of frenzy in the air. Or rather a mixture of frenzies. The huntsmen were frantic to fight back; the SOBs were frantic to kill them all.

When the final trooper fell to Billy Two's commandeered blade, the five Soldiers of Barrabas and their white-haired leader regrouped in the middle of the barracks. Death was all around them. The room was strewn with contorted bodies, blood-drenched sheets, red-dripping walls and the stench of exploded bowels.

Barrabas didn't have to say anything about their success; congratulations were not in order.

"Let's get their weapons," he told the others, bending down and picking up a dropped Makarov from the floor. "Knives, too."

Nate wiped the gore from a pistol's plastic grip with the end of a sheet.

"No time to get things tidy, Beck," O'Toole told him. "Shove it in your coat and let's roll."

Beck was the last one out of the room. He shut out the lights before he closed the door. The afterimage of the havoc they had wrought burned into his retina. The SOBs made their way down to the first floor. Either the flight crew of the Ilyushin were used to hearing a lot of racket from the *spetsnaz* contingent or the scuffling and crashing had not been audible on the lower floors. The pilot had a room all to himself. It wasn't a big room. Not much larger than the closet in which Lee had dealt with Balandin. It seemed even smaller when all six American mercenaries slipped in through the unlocked door. In the light of a floodlight streaming through the unshaded window they could see their new conscript fast asleep.

The pilot awakened with a start as the cold snout of a Makarov nuzzled into his right ear.

"No noise!" Lee told him in Russian.

Liam turned on the room lights.

The pilot looked like he was about to burst into tears.

"Put on your pants," Lee said. "Do as we say and you won't be hurt."

The Russian got dressed quickly.

Billy Two shoved his coat at him, then shoved him at the door.

"I don't like his vibes," Barrabas whispered to Lee. "He looks like a rabbit about to bolt. We need him functional."

"I'll see to it," she said.

As the other SOBs filed out of the dorm room, Dr. Hatton had a short word with the pilot. She told him that they had already killed more than a dozen armed *spetsnaz* upstairs, showed him the captured guns to prove it, and added that at the first sign of resistance on his part, an attempt to escape, to thwart their plans, he would be swiftly and thoroughly disemboweled. To drive her point home, she prodded him the whole time she spoke just under the point of his sternum with the needle-sharp tip of a commando knife.

It was a sober and philosophical pilot who exited the room ahead of the woman doctor. A man ready to fly for a new flag.

The skull and crossbones.

The SOBs left the dormitory building by the front doors, moving across the icy sidewalk to the curb, where a black Lada four-door sedan was parked.

The street, though well-lighted, was completely deserted. Ust Tavda rolled over and played dead after ten at night.

O'Toole applied the sole of his boot to the Lada's front passenger-side window. The glass spider-webbed but held. He kicked a second time and caved in the safety pane.

Barrabas reached in and opened the door.

The SOBs piled into the car. Barrabas made the pilot get behind the wheel. The white-haired man sat in the front seat by the shattered window. He reached across Lee's lap to hot-wire the engine, jerking the harness of ignition wires free from under the dash. The Lada growled to life.

"Tell our friend we want to go to the airfield," Barrabas told her. "Tell him if the airport-gate security people get suspicious he'll be the first to die."

Lee smiled. "He already knows that, but it never hurts to repeat a threat," she said, whipping out her commando knife and jabbing it lightly into the man's side. "Drive. And do it carefully. Very carefully," she told the pilot in Russian.

The man revved the engine and pulled the overloaded sedan away from the curb.

"What if we get hassled at the gate, Colonel?" Beck asked.

Barrabas looked over into the back seat, the expression on his face as cold as the subarctic night. "If we get stopped, we shoot it out. We've got no other choice at this stage. We can't explain how we got out of the dorm without an escort, and if the airport guys try and call to check up, somebody's bound to walk into that room full of dead troopers. We are past the point of no return."

The SOBs rode in silence, each thinking his or her own thoughts as the bleak scenery rolled by the windows, the empty public squares, heaps of snow piled up in the gutters by a city snowplow, the towering modern buildings streaming light from almost every window. The Russians still awake were busy worrying about their kids' teeth, their mother-in-law, the foreman at the plant, wondering if they were ever going to see another roll of decent toilet paper, taste another fresh orange. The Party people had no worries, except to maintain control, to keep the rest of the population quietly wanting, submissive, afraid.

"I wish you had a lighter touch, O'Toole," Beck said, his teeth chattering. The night air was flooding in through the destroyed window.

"Or a smaller foot," Billy Two added.

"You guys are some pair of heroes," Liam said. "You don't see me or Dayo complaining, do you?"

Dayo answered for himself. "The Eskimo can't complain. He's frozen."

"Shut up," Barrabas warned them as they drew near to the airport gate. "Only the pilot and doc talk. If things get nasty, she'll give the green light. Get your guns ready."

"Just watch where you're shootin'," Billy Two said to the other three in the back seat. "Remember, I'm between your muzzles and the target."

"Shut up!"

The security guards stepped out of their Quonset hut as the pilot stopped the Lada in front of the closed wire gate. The guards had AK-74s slung on shoulder straps. Their fists were wrapped around the grips, fingers resting outside trigger guards.

Lee said something to the pilot as the gateman gestured for him to roll down his window.

The pilot produced a sheaf of identification documents from inside his coat. He also must've said something funny to the guards because they started laughing. Lee turned to the SOBs and repeated the unintelligible phrase. Barrabas and the rest joined in on the merriment.

When the chuckles died down, things got tense. One of the guards pointed at the mass of masculinity in the back seat and asked a question. The pilot talked a mile a minute. Lee's knife was spurring him to new heights of elocution.

The curious guard conferred with his partner. When he turned back to the car, he was grinning. And nodding agreement.

They unlocked the wire gate and the pilot drove the Lada onto the airfield.

"What did he say?" O'Toole asked.

Lee spoke without turning. "He told those bozos we were unloading some contraband cargo from the Ilyushin. He offered to give them a share on our way out."

"What did he tell 'em we had? Record albums?"

"No. Dirty magazines."

"Heav-ee," Billy Two said.

The pilot parked the Lada at the foot of the Ilyushin's gang way.

"Tell him he did a good job," Barrabas said.

"He knows it," O'Toole said from the back seat. "He's still alive, isn't he?"

"Just don't tell him what we're about to do," Dayo added. "We wouldn't want to ruin his evening."

"Better go ahead and get him into the plane, Lee," Barrabas said. "You go along, too, Chank. School is in session as of right now."

There was no security on the hangar where the supposedly empty test-equipment crates were stored. The SOBs opened one of the huge sliding doors and entered.

"Get the lights," Barrabas said.

When Billy Two found the switch and they could see what they were doing, they attacked the false bottoms of the crates with crowbars and screwdrivers they found on the hangar's workbench. In a couple of minutes, they had the bottoms ripped up and were passing out Soviet small arms. Each mercenary took an AK-74 and a handful of extra 30-round magazines. There were also a pair of Dragunov sniper rifles, some RPGs and assorted ComBloc grenades.

"Let's get the jamming gear out," Barrabas said, shouldering an AK and RPG.

They carefully removed the electronics from the bottom of the box.

"I hope it didn't get screwed up on the way from Riga," Nate said.

"No shit," Billy Two exclaimed. "If these gulag goons call for help and get it, we're not going to celebrate New Year's."

"Not this year. Not ever again," Barrabas said.

The SOBs carried their assault gear up the gangway and into the transport, stacking it in the aisle.

The pilot stood in the cockpit doorway and stared at the weapons and ammunition, a look of pure horror on his face. He was beginning to get the picture. And it scared the holy hell out of him.

"Have we got a problem, Colonel?" O'Toole asked, jerking a thumb at the petrified pilot.

Lee answered his question. She grabbed the man by the back of the collar and spun him around, facing the pilot's seat. She shouted something at him, then shoved him to his place. He sat down and started flipping switches.

"What did you tell him?" Liam asked.

"I said we were going to Disneyworld via Siberia, and if he wanted to shake hands with Mickey and Donald he'd better be a good boy."

"Hey, Doc," Dayo called from the copilot's seat, "you better get in here and start translating. This guy's lost me already."

Lee turned back to the cockpit.

The SOBs had just finished battening down their gear when she returned to the passenger cabin. "Flight check is complete, Colonel. We're ready to go."

Barrabas grimaced. He was counting on luck again. Counting on the guys at the gate not to call in an alarm, a scramble of jet interceptors that would end the mission and leave his team thousands of kilometers short of their goal.

"Roll it," he said.

18

Anatoly Leonov shivered on the floor of the darkened mess hall. Too weak to rise. Too weak to return to the barracks. There were others on the floor with him. Others struggling to draw breath. Fighting against their own will to live. The final sufferings of the goners had no reason, served no glorious and noble cause. Freedom was, in the end, the bitch of bitches. Demanding all, yielding nothing.

Around his eyes, in his throat and his nose there was intense heat. Heat from within. It burned his lips, his nostrils, his tongue, this fever raging inside. He wanted water with all his soul, but he would not, could not, drag himself across the wooden floor. He was afraid of the dark in the corner where the water bucket stood, afraid he would never make it there or never make it back. Oddly, he took comfort from the presence of his *dokhodyaga* brethren. His moans were theirs. Their wild, desperate thoughts were his. A union of pain. Of heartbreak.

The scientist considered how hard he had struggled to live over the past two years. How even when mortally hurt, he had fought to keep from being drowned in the wash bucket. For what? Drowning was an easy way out. The shock of water in the lungs made the central nervous system shut down. One blacked out after a moment of discomfort and never woke up. Even now, knowing full well that he was doomed, he could not give up. Even though he felt as if he was being drawn down in slow motion to the pit of hell, as if the merciful moment of pain in a drowning death was stretched and stretched until it encompassed an entire lifetime, ten lifetimes.

His cheek was resting on the floor. He heard the rumble of footsteps coming toward him from the dark, but he could not raise his head to see who it was. He closed his eyes. They burned like hot coals against his eyelids.

The wet toe of a felt boot nudged his chin.

"Do you know what day it is, famous comrade?" said a gruff voice from above.

Leonov did not understand the question. The string of words made no sense to him.

Kruzhkov planted the sole of his boot on the prostrate man's temple and rocked his head back and forth on the floor, bearing down just enough to make his victim whimper.

"Famous comrade, today is your dying day. And my lucky day. You will have finally done one useful thing in your life: you will have won me three hundred rubles."

The pain brought Leonov back from the fever

daze. He tried to speak, but his tongue stuck to the roof of his mouth. So dry, so very dry.

"I know what you're thinking," Kruzhkov said, shifting his boot back to the floor and kneeling down. "You're thinking the others will never pay up because they'll know I killed you." The trusty laughed softly. "They might know, but they won't be able to prove it."

He scooped up the emaciated man in his powerful arms and turned for the door.

When Kruzhkov stepped out into the frigid night air, his human burden began to tremble violently. The cold sucked away the last of Leonov's strength, sucked it from the marrow of his bones.

"You will be found in a few hours," Kruzhkov said, setting the scientist down in the snow halfway between the mess hall and the entrance to the prisoners' barracks. "Everyone will think you tried to crawl back to your bunk and didn't make it. A convenient stroke of luck for me."

Leonov curled up into a tight ball on his side.

"Brrr," Kruzhkov said, stamping his feet. "My warm bed calls me. Thank you, famous comrade, for lasting this long. I knew you could do it. Good night. And goodbye."

19

Chank Dayo's butt was stuck to the copilot's seat. Stuck from sweat. Mastering the controls of the transport plane was not the kind of thing to rush, yet rush it had to be. The Ilyushin covered the fifty klicks between Ust Tavda and the Tarkotovo gulag complex in fifteen minutes. Of those fifteen, Dayo solo-piloted the craft for about ten.

"How's it going up here?" Barrabas said, leaning in the cockpit entryway.

"We've got a visual on the camp," Lee said. "It's straight ahead less than two kilometers."

"Getting the hang of it, Chank?" Billy Two asked over the colonel's shoulder. Like the rest of the SOBs and their leader, Billy was dressed for winter combat: white camou shroud over his parka, white puttees over his boots, white camou tape over the length of his AK-74.

"He'd goddamn better have," Barrabas said. "We're going to circle that airstrip once. Then we're going in. Doc, it's time for the Mayday." As Lee pulled the hand mike off its overhead rack, Barrabas called to Beck who was stationed at the first row of seats. "Jam time, Nate. Give 'em hell as soon as the doc signs off."

Beck nodded, bending over the battery-powered, wide-band jammer. It was already humming, warmed up and ready to confuse and confound.

Lee pressed the transmit button and rattled off a standard air-distress call. Then without waiting for ground confirmation of message, added that they were out of fuel and coming down, to prepare for a crash landing.

"Hit it, Beck!" Barrabas shouted as Lee switched off the transmit.

In the seconds before the Ilyushin's receiver was choked with static and whistles, someone from the camp responded.

"What did he say?" Barrabas asked.

"I only got a couple of words," Lee said. "He wanted a repeat of the message."

Barrabas stared out the windscreen. The sky was black, the ground was white and on the horizon line ahead a mound of twinkling lights appeared. "One time around," he told Dayo.

The Eskimo eased back on the engines' power and slipped the transport into a low, slow left turn. As they neared the airstrip, he banked right. They could see one pair of truck headlights, then another, rushing from the camp gates, barreling down the road to the strip.

"Our welcoming committee," Lee said. "Look, they're lighting the runway lamps."

As Chank completed his turn, the runway crew finished firing the oil lamps. The SOBs and their unwilling passenger got their first good look at the primitive airstrip.

The pilot let out a shrill cry and started waving his hands wildly. *"Nyet! Nyet!"* he shouted, grabbing the wheel in front of him, trying to take control of the plane away from Dayo.

"What's with him?" Billy said.

"It's the ice," Lee said. "He says we can't land this plane on that strip."

"He's in for a big surprise, huh, Chank?" the Indian said.

Dayo didn't answer his friend's question. "The landing gear, dammit!" he said. "Have that commie bastard lower the frigging wheels!"

Lee put the muzzle of her Makarov to the man's temple and repeated the order in Russian.

The landing gear locked down just as Dayo began his final approach.

"I suggest," the Eskimo said, a slight tremor in his baritone voice, "that everybody buckle up."

The SOBs hurried to their seats and fastened safety belts.

Dayo knew that he was going to need every inch of the airstrip to stop the Ilyushin, so he used it. He set the rear wheels down so close to the landing edge of the runway that the man in the pilot's seat fainted. As the nose wheel touched down, he feathered the brakes.

Mistake.

The transport did not slow down but began to drift ever so slightly sideways; the view from the cockpit window shifted away from the main gulag and toward the empty blackness of the horizon.

"Oh, shit!" somebody in the passenger section cried.

The Ilyushin was a third of the way down the runway, and its air speed was still over a hundred miles an hour. Dayo knew what would happen if he didn't slow the plane down: it would end up in a ball of fire somewhere out in the middle of the frozen marsh. He clamped down on the brakes, and the slight drift instantly became more pronounced.

"Shit!" came the shout from behind.

Just don't flip! Dayo prayed. Don't flip!

The tail of the plane was passing the nose, moving with an unhurried grace.

"Time to pucker up, folks," O'Toole shouted over the steady groan of the brakes. "And kiss your asses goodbye."

The plane made one complete revolution, then slowed noticeably. Through the windscreen, Chank could see the warning lamps the gulag crew had set out at the extreme end of the runway. They were sliding toward them, even though the speed was falling back.

"It's gonna be tight," he shouted. "Real tight."

The Ilyushin stopped with a violent shudder.

Half of its right wing hung over the end line of the airstrip.

"Some flyer, huh?" Billy said to O'Toole, giving him a solid nudge of the elbow.

"You Amerinds are all out of your minds."

"Shake it," Barrabas said, jumping up from his seat, picking up his AK. "We wait for them to move the ramp up...."

"Hey, Colonel, there isn't any ramp," Beck said.

Barrabas moved to a window. "Jesus!" he said. It was true. The airstrip was too small and too primitive to have a standard mobile stairway.

"They're pulling that covered six by six up under the front door," Liam said.

"That'll have to do," Barrabas said. "Liam, you and Billy will handle the RPG chores. Wait until we clear the airstrip around the plane, then hit the two closest gun towers. They're the only ones that can do the plane any harm. We'll regroup after we have control of the field."

The white-haired man surveyed the rest of his troops. Beck, Lee and Dayo stood by the front door, AKs in hand.

"The faster we move the better," he told them. "We've got to capitalize on our element of surprise. We're not going to have it for long. Jump onto the truck's canopy, then down in between it and the plane. Come around the truck shooting. Don't let anybody drive off in the other truck. We need it."

Outside, the driver of the truck parked under the plane's front door gave his horn a honk.

"Show time, once again," Barrabas said. His AK made a dry clack as he thumbed the fire selector lever to full-auto. "Open the goddamn door."

Dayo cracked the hatch, then cranked the heavy door back.

As soon as it was all the way open, Barrabas jumped, dropping the five feet to the roof of the six by six. The KGB prison guards waved at him enthusiastically. It was understandable. They thought the Ilyushin had just survived a crash landing. They thought they were heroes. They didn't pay any attention to the weapon the big man carried so casually.

Barrabas stepped down onto the hood of the truck and from there to the ground. Above him, there was another clunk of boots hitting the roof of the truck cab. He moved to the rear of the vehicle. Another clunk. And another.

One of the KGB men shouted something.

Barrabas rounded the back bumper of the truck, the AK-74 balanced between his big hands. He swept his sights across the ragged line of men, swept and pinned the trigger. The tight and compact weapon bucked obediently, spitting 5.45mm lead, sending the assembled bluecaps spinning, diving, crashing to the icy runway.

The clatter of autofire signaled the end of deception. Beck and Lee opened up from the front of the truck, using the heavy bumper as a shield. Lee poked the snout of her AK over the top of the truck's passenger door and unloaded three semiauto rounds into the dumbfounded driver. He died leaning on the horn. Its unbroken wail blended in with the screams of the KGB guards. Screams of surprise, outrage. They hadn't come properly dressed for a firefight. All they carried were their side arms. Makarovs popped frantically as they tried to retreat in some semblance of order.

Beck emptied one 30-round clip and started on a second. The shriek of answering fire overhead, 9mm slugs skipping off the ice, clanging off the truck bumper, set his blood pounding, but he had enough self-control to flip his AK selector switch to semiauto to conserve ammunition.

Chank, meanwhile, dropped to his belly and slid under the truck where he was shooting from a prone position. He pressed the trigger, felt the slight buck of recoil and watched his target topple. Even before the man hit the ice, Dayo was searching for a new victim. They weren't so easy to find. The ice was littered with fallen men. Only one moved. Ran. His back to the plane, his legs pumping, he fought the slippery footing. Dayo put the post of the AK front sight on the small of the guard's back and squeezed off a round.

Three other SOBs chose the same target. At almost precisely the same instant. Not one, but four 5.45mm tumblers slammed the running man. He dropped to his face and slid a good thirty feet before coming to a stop. A dead stop.

"We got 'em, Colonel," Beck shouted.

"All right, O'Toole, Starfoot," Barrabas yelled up at the plane. "Get down here."

The two men jumped onto the truck with Dragunovs shouldered and RPGs in their hands. They didn't hop down to the ground but knelt where they were, Billy Two on top of the truck roof, Liam on the hood. The distance was about a thousand meters up a slight incline because of the hill. Their targets were clearly outlined by the camp's klieg lights. There was no wisecracking now. Both Billy and Liam knew the gun towers were manned, that the gunners had put in plenty of practice time shooting downhill toward the airstrip. They probably had the ranges preset. And now they were standing up there, wondering what the hell was going on, waiting for an order to open fire. They would be waiting an eternity.

The SOBs were experts with rocket-propelled grenades. The two tubes whooshed, belching yellow flame from behind. The rockets tracked a straight line, true up slope. The two gun towers exploded simultaneously. One of them was blown completely off its stanchions; of the other only the supporting platform remained, swept clean of heavy machine gun, clean of humanity.

Suddenly it was quiet, except for the wailing of the truck's horn.

Barrabas jerked the driver door open and hauled the dead man off the button, dumping him out onto the ground. "Get that other truck started," he told Billy. "You and Dayo follow the rest of us." He waved for Liam, Lee and Beck as he climbed behind the bloody steering wheel.

Lee and Nate jumped in the cab, and O'Toole hopped on the running board. The white-haired man gunned the engine and jammed it into gear. With a series of short violent jerks the six by six leaped into motion.

"If our luck is still holding," Barrabas shouted over the truck's roar, "the guards at the main camp won't know if we're their own guys trying to get back to safety or an attacking force. Once we turn for the satellite camp they're not going to have any doubts. We're bound to run into some head-on fire on the way back."

Barrabas stopped the truck halfway up the road that linked the airstrip with the two camps. Billy Two stopped right behind him. The colonel piled out and ran back to Billy's truck.

"You can see the other front-facing gun tower from here," he said, pointing it out. "It's got to go before we make the turn to the satellite camp."

"No problem."

"You guys will wait here. Keep the main camp force from pursuing us. Keep them pinned down inside the perimeter."

"Understood, Colonel," Billy said.

Barrabas trotted back to the lead truck, jumped in and set off for the road leading to the satellite camp.

As they approached the intersecting road a clatter of heavy machine-gun fire erupted from the camp to their left. Slugs gnawed at the icy track ahead of them.

"Come on, Starfoot," Barrabas growled, jamming the gas pedal to the floor, "don't fail me now."

20

Billy Two lined up the RPG's sights with the gun tower. The gunners were already firing on the lead truck. He could hear the staccato thunder of full-auto reports, see the winking flame.

"Shoot, man, shoot!" Dayo said.

Billy let her rip.

The rocket streaked up toward its target, climbing along a draftsman's line, point *A* to point *B*. With a brilliant flash of orange and a solid *crump*, point *B* ceased to exist.

Billy ducked back down behind the hood of the truck as small-arms fire from the main camp's gate sizzled overhead. It also connected with the truck body; the impact of lead on steel sent quivers through the chassis and blew out the front windshield and headlights.

"Man, they are screwing up the trade-in value," Dayo said, keeping his head low.

Billy reloaded the launcher. "They're going to catch the others broadside if we don't do something about it."

He raised up again, braving the hail of steel-cored

slugs and sighted on the camp gates. His angle of attack was oblique and the gates themselves were built of heavy timbers lashed together, stockade style. He wasn't hoping to annihilate the enemy, just to make them shrink back from the entrance until the truck had passed.

The launcher shuddered, and its payload was away. It streaked past the truck Barrabas was driving, and angled off to the left. The right side of the gatepost disintegrated, as did a section of stockade fence and those KGB men unlucky enough to be hiding behind it.

The racing truck cleared the right-hand turn and sped down the gradual slope toward the marsh bridge and the satellite camp gate.

Billy slumped back behind the cover of the truck.

"How many do you think you got?" Chank asked.

Bullets started whining overhead again and slamming into the opposite side of the truck.

"Not nearly enough," Billy said, putting down the RPG and picking up his Dragunov.

Multiple hits on the left front tire dropped the truck's front end on that side.

"Time to go to work," he said, easing out around the bumper, the Soviet sniper rifle's sling strap tightly wrapped around his supporting arm. He pressed the 4-power scope's rubber eyecup to his eye, found a head peering out around the gate and squeezed off a round. The Dragunov bucked with

authority. No piddling 5.45mm slug, but a
7.92mm. It hit with authority, too. Billy watched
as the owner of the head cartwheeled out from behind his cover, landing in a heap in the exposed
gateway.

Dayo, too, got busy. An experienced warrior, he
knew better than to shoot over the hood of the
truck. Bullets could be easily skipped right into
him. The best cover was taken, so he had to make
do with the rear end, the back bumper. There
wasn't the bullet-stopping bulk of engine block, but
there were steel wheels and double-wall body con-
struction.

Chank swung out and popped off three rounds
semiauto, then swung back. He couldn't tell if he'd
hit anything, but he was sure he was bracketing the
kill zone.

Up at the front of the truck, the Dragunov barked
twice.

Dayo swung out again and sent four more rounds
up toward the camp gate. He ducked back and
waited for the answering fire to clang into the truck.
There was none.

Seconds dragged on.

The Eskimo was suddenly aware of how cold he
was, thanks to the sweat sticking his shirt to his
back. He also started thinking about his vision.
Looked back at the plane, at the burning landing
lights, at the oil drums. It wasn't exactly the same,
but it was close enough to make him shudder. The

feeling of doom, of futility slipped over him. He fought against it. If he was to die there, if there was nothing he could do to change that fact, then at least he could go out like a man.

"Oh, Jesus!" Billy groaned from up near the bumper.

Chank heard the sound of an engine. He peered out around the back end and saw the source. The KGB men had another six by six in the camp. They had loaded it up and were driving it out the gate.

"This way, you assholes!" Billy snarled, stepping out from behind the cover of the truck, firing a steady string of single shots.

Dayo jumped out, too. Flipping his fire selector to full auto, he dumped half a magazine in the general direction of the truck.

The vehicle veered hard right.

"It worked, goddamnit!" Billy cried. "The bastards are coming for us, not the colonel."

"Yeah, great," Chank said, cracking in a fresh mag, yanking the operating handle and jacking a live round into the chamber. "What the hell are we going to do, now?"

"I knew you were going to ask that question," Billy Two said.

A SUDDEN BLAZE OF LIGHT and an earsplitting boom signaled the end of the gun tower.

"All right, Billy!" Barrabas said, slowing down to take the sharp turn. As he did so, the main camp's gate to his left opened and a dozen assault rifles crackled, sending bullets whining into the side of the truck.

There was no way to return fire.

"Keep your heads down!" the colonel growled, squashing the gas pedal, steering the lumbering six by six around the corner.

Again a flash of light and a blistering whack of HE.

In his side mirror Barrabas saw the gatepost fly into the air with a couple of guards and parts thereof. He really tromped on it, then, pedal to the metal on the slight downward incline. Ahead, he could see the bridge over the marsh and the lights of Slash One.

Slash One could see them, too.

Heavy machine-gun fire ripped across the center of the icy road. Both of the gun towers guarding the road were shooting, drawing a line of death and daring the SOBs to cross it.

Barrabas stopped the truck just before the wooden bridge, just beyond the accurate range of the towers. "Take 'em out, Liam," he said.

The Irishman unslung the RPG from his back, stepped off the running board and dropped to a kneeling position. As he did so, the machine-gun slugs skipped forward, over the wooden bridge, splintering the boards and chewing up the road.

"Shit, they've raised their guns!" Beck exclaimed.

Liam pressed the trigger. The rocket whooshed away. Half the camp's frontal firepower vanished in a blur of light and smoke. The thunder-crack report came to them a second later.

Bullets from the remaining tower clawed the frozen earth, pummeling it like rain from hell.

O'Toole reloaded his launcher.

"Hurry up," Lee told him as he shouldered the weapon.

"Nag, nag," the red-haired man said, sighting down the short tube and squeezing the trigger.

Rocket engine ignited. Flame gushed from the exhaust port. Then the green beauty was away. It bore a special message for the occupants of gun tower number two. A message of doom.

The tower fragmented under the HE blast. A skeleton on stilts, burning, collapsing in on itself.

"The front gates," Barrabas said.

O'Toole repacked the firing tube and unleashed another dose of destruction. The satellite camp's wire outer gates came apart. A second shot from the RPG cracked one of the wooden gates off its hinges.

"Not bad shooting, huh, Colonel?" Liam said.

"Keep it up and I'll pin another medal on you," the white-haired man said as he slipped the truck into gear.

"Make it a quart of Bushmill's and I'll see what I can do," O'Toole said as he climbed back up on the running board of the moving vehicle.

"You're on."

Barrabas gunned the engine, forcing the six by six to pick up speed. They thundered over the wooden bridge and into a withering barrage of small-arms fire from the camp's blasted gates. The front windshield spiderwebbed.

"Oh, God," Beck moaned.

Barrabas drove on.

21

Anatoly Leonov was speaking with his dear friend Valentin when the air exploded with sustained bursts of machine-gun fire. Then flashes of light so brilliant he could see them even with his eyes tightly closed, see them right through his eyelids. He was lightly pelted by a fall of rain.

This was no storm of nature.

Thunder and lightning were creatures of the Siberian spring, not the winter.

The mental image of his friend, once so vivid, so comforting, began to crumble. And the harder he tried to hold it, the faster it fell apart.

All around him there was the tramp of running footsteps.

Someone kicked him and dashed on.

Leonov opened his eyes and saw the burning, gutted gun towers. He saw that the curious rain was not made of water but of bits of flesh from the exploded bodies of the tower gunners. With a great effort he managed to turn himself to face the camp gates. There was a line of guards there, and they were shooting their rifles at something out on the road.

The ground rocked.

The world winked white.

There was a terrible boom.

Leonov covered his face with his hands.

It was raining again. Heavier this time. Bigger chunks.

He blinked away the dirt from his eyes and stared at the camp gates, blown off their hinges. Who would do such a thing? Who in a country of contented, enslaved sheep would risk the terrible wrath of the ruling Party by attacking one of its most venerable institutions?

The question had an answer. No one.

This, Leonov decided, is part of the fever. Or perhaps I am already dead.

BILLY TWO SNAPPED A FULL MAG into his Dragunov.

"Shoot the goddamn driver!" he said, leaning on the bullet-pocked front fender, drawing a bead on the right side of the windshield of the onrushing truck.

Dayo stepped out from behind cover, too. Cover would be no use to them if a truckload of angry KGB men got within striking distance of the escape plane.

They opened up in unison. Billy punched single shots from the semiauto sniper rifle, and Chank fired short bursts. It was the Dragunov that did the real damage. Heavier slugs. Tighter groups. Billy slammed a half-dozen shots through the glass above the steering wheel.

The truck kept on coming.

"Kill him!" Billy cried, firing another three through the same crusty aperture.

Chank did his best with what was basically a short-range weapon. He sprayed the passenger section of the windshield, the radiator, the headlights.

Like a goddamn express train, the truck did not swerve, waver or slow down.

Both the SOBs saw the same thing in the same instant.

Through the bullet-riddled windshield, they saw dead bodies. Heads blasted, shattered like mannequins, the inside of the cab glistening with gore. Behind the wheel was one of the newly departed. Dead, he was lead-footing it, pinning the gas pedal to the floorboards.

"Jump!" Billy hollered, diving away from the side of the truck an instant before impact.

Dayo was way ahead of him. The Eskimo had already rolled and was coming up on his feet when the two trucks collided.

The impact was colossal.

It sent the stationary truck skidding backward on the ice.

It stopped the moving truck cold.

Doors flew off. Wheels flew off. Bodies flew off. Dead ones from the cab. Live ones from the bed.

The KGB guards crashed to earth with their weapons. Some just lay there, unmoving. Others came up shooting.

There was no cover except for the trucks, and the two SOBs were positioned so none of their enemies could reach safety. Unfortunately the same was true for them. Belly down on the hard frozen ground, Billy and Chank shot back. Shot across the gap of no more than thirty feet.

The sniper scope was, of course, useless. As were the iron sights of the AK. It was point and pull. And pray.

Dayo emptied one clip and clawed another from his outer shell pocket. Billy was still popping off single shots as he rammed the mag home and activated the operating handle. Then the shooting stopped.

Dark forms lay sprawled on the white ground. Nothing moved. Nothing even moaned.

"You gonna go check 'em out?" Chank said.

The idea of turning over a live one playing possum did not appeal to either of them.

"I'll flip you for it."

"I can't see the coin from here."

"I can't get into my pants pockets, anyway. Pick a number between one and ten."

"You've got to be kidding."

"No, go on. I wouldn't cheat an old buddy like you. Go on, pick a number."

"Six."

"You lose."

"Bullshit."

"All right, we do it together," Billy said. "But

keep your damned eyes open. I don't like the idea of getting shot in the back.''

"You and me both.''

The two SOBs rose cautiously from their prone positions and crawled to the nearest clump of bodies. They quickly sorted through the tangle of arms and legs and, finding no pulses, no breathing, moved on.

"Wouldn't it be great if they were all dead and we had nothing to worry about?'' Billy said as he reached down to take a pulse under a supine man's jawline.

The KGB guard waited until the Indian touched him before he whipped out his automatic pistol.

"Shit! Shit!'' Billy cried, jerking back as the handgun barked. Hot lead whistled past the tip of his aquiline nose.

Dayo thrust his AK forward, firing it with a one-hand hold on the pistol grip, stitching the man's torso from crotch to throat with close to thirty rounds of lead.

"Oh, man, I hate that surprise-I-gotcha shit,'' Billy said. "Spooks the hell out of me.''

"There is a way around it,'' Chank said.

"Yeah, why not?'' Billy said.

The two of them started potshotting corpses or make-believe corpses. Sure as hell, three of the "dead'' guys jumped up and made a break for the trucks.

They never got there.

22

Liam O'Toole hung on to the truck's passenger door with his left hand and shot the AK with his right, returning the fire of the men crouching at the camp entrance. The bouncing of the truck made precise aiming impossible. O'Toole dumped one mag in a single burst, then jammed the weapon butt-first to Lee.

She didn't reload and pass his gun back; she passed him hers, already loaded, cocked and unlocked.

As the distance to the camp gates narrowed, Liam found the mark. Bullet tracks from the second AK stitched all around and among the defenders, who either fell or fell back.

"Look at 'em run!" O'Toole shouted. "Look at the bastards run!"

The withering siege of fire quickly dwindled to a ragged and halfhearted flurry.

"We're going straight through, Liam," Barrabas yelled. "Get your ass inside the cab!"

The red-haired man climbed through the window, headfirst, onto the laps of Beck and Dr. Hatton just as Barrabas rolled over the fallen wire outer fence. The ravaged inner gates rushed up at them and their leader hit the brakes.

The six by six skidded through the opening and into the gulag yard, where it slewed to a stop. Men in rags scattered every which way. Running. Limping. Crawling. Steel-cored slugs hammered on the truck's hood.

"Out!" Barrabas said. "Bail out!"

He kicked his door open and dived away from the truck, rolling, coming up with his AK ready to rip. Beck, Hatton and O'Toole jumped out the other side.

More gunfire erupted from deeper in the compound. Barrabas located its source. Between the rear two camp buildings. He did a quick body count of the bluecaps around him. Of the fifteen men supposedly stationed at the satellite camp, twelve were already dead.

Using hand signals, he pointed out the last defenders to his SOBs. He also indicated the attack plan. The others would sweep right; he would sweep left. Unless the KGB men could fly, there was no place for them to go.

The three-person team closed in with precision, leapfrogging, applying pressure, until it forced the KGB men to retreat. To retreat right into Barrabas's sights.

He cut them down in one long burst of fire, the AK chugging as he shot from the hip.

The other three ran up to him as he reloaded.

Beck was ecstatic. "I don't believe this," he said. "I don't believe we've actually come this far without getting our noses bloody."

"We'd better get on with it," Lee said, gesturing at the grimy faces on the other side of the equally grimy barracks' windows. "We've got to find our man in all this mess."

For the first time Barrabas allowed himself to see the camp as something other than a kill zone. He had seen a lot of prisons, many of them from the inside, but he had never seen anything worse than Slash One. It was a shanty town on a bed of frozen muck. It had a smell all its own. A mixture of garbage dump and burning wood. And it was inhabited by human scarecrows. Filthy human scarecrows.

The white-haired man turned to his mercenaries and said, "Get 'em all out of the buildings. Get 'em out on the double!"

Beck, Lee and O'Toole banged on ramshackle doors and windows, shouting at the terrified prisoners. Only when they discharged some ammunition into the ceilings did the men obey. They shuffled out onto the frozen central quad, eyes round, huge, doll-like.

"Tell them no one is going to hurt them," Barrabas ordered the doctor. As she spoke, he saw that not all the prisoners were in such bad shape. Some of them were actually plump. These hung to the back of the crowd, trying to avoid close scrutiny.

"Ask them where Anatoly Leonov is."

Lee repeated the question in Russian.

No one answered.

"Tell them we are his friends."

She did so.

The scarecrows looked at the ground.

Then a hand raised in the back row. A firm, fleshy hand. "I know where he is," the prisoner said in Russian.

"Have that guy step forward," Barrabas said.

There was a rumbling among the crowd as Kruzhkov elbowed his way to the front. The trusty told Lee his name and said he knew where to find "his dear comrade" Leonov.

More grumbling issued from the crowd. Especially from the skinniest and dirtiest of the lot.

"This way," Kruzhkov said, gesturing for the SOBs to follow.

In fact, the whole prisoner population followed. They didn't have far to go. Anatoly Leonov was curled up beside an open latrine.

Dr. Hatton bent over the emaciated man, her fingers searching for and finding a pulse. "He's alive, Nile. But only barely."

Barrabas addressed the assembled camp in English. "Is this Anatoly Leonov?" His meaning was clear to all. And all nodded or grunted assent.

The plump man who had located the scientist leaned down alongside Lee and said, "If you are taking him to freedom, you must take me, too. We are the closest of friends."

"Liar!" said someone in the crowd.

"Bitch!"

"Murderer!"

Leonov opened his eyes and looked up at Lee's face, framed by the camou white outer shell. "Are you an angel?" he asked, his voice a failing whisper.

"Dear comrade," Kruzhkov said over her shoulder, "you have me to thank for saving your life. I led your rescuers to you. You will take me away when you leave."

The prisoners of conscience in the crowd, long-suffering, long victimized, had reached the breaking point. They surged forward in a solid mass and before the SOBs could do anything to prevent it they dragged Kruzhkov back.

"Stop! Stop or I'll fire!" Lee said, swinging up the muzzle of her AK.

"Go ahead and shoot," one of the prisoners said. "Give us a clean, swift death. And revenge!"

Kruzhkov screamed from the middle of the pack, buried under the press of bodies. Over the top of the crowd, from hand to hand, lengths of stout timber were passed. In the center of the knot of humanity, the tips of the clubs rose and fell and as they did the plump prisoner shrieked high and shrill.

"They're going to kill him," Lee said.

No sooner were the words out of her mouth than the beating stopped. The screaming continued, however.

"Get back!" she said, shoving the men aside. They parted for her, shuffling away from the fallen prisoner.

Kruzhkov sat flat on the frozen mud, his legs bent at the knees, bent the way no knee was ever meant to go.

"Christ, they've shattered both his kneecaps," Lee said. "He'll never walk again."

"Or murder!" shouted a prisoner.

"Or eat other men!"

Barrabas scooped Leonov up from the ground. "You've seen the last of this place," he said.

The scientist struggled out of his delirium. "No, I can't go!" he protested in English. "I can't go and leave my brothers here."

Barrabas gave Dr. Hatton an incredulous look.

"If you won't take them along, put me down," Leonov said. "I choose to die among them."

"We've got room, Nile," Lee said.

"For all of them?" Beck asked, viewing the legion of starved and unwashed.

"Not all of them," the white-haired man said. "If there are more scumbags like our 'dear comrade' there in the dirt, they stay behind."

"How can we tell which of the prisoners deserve freedom?" Lee asked the scientist.

He smiled a distant smile. "Take only the skinny ones," he said. "Only the very skinny ones."

Then Leonov's head slumped.

Lee took another pulse. "He's fading on us. We've got to get him to the plane where it's warm or we're going to lose him for sure."

"Okay, okay, Doc," Barrabas said, carrying the scientist over to the truck. He gently laid the man in the covered bed. "Beck, O'Toole, you're in charge of travel arrangements. Check all the buildings, make sure you don't leave anybody too weak to walk behind. Get cracking!"

"All right, guys," Liam shouted to the assembled prisoners, "show us your bones!"

Nine men beside Leonov either climbed under their own power or were carried into the bed of the truck. The rest of the prisoners Beck locked in the largest of the barracks buildings.

Barrabas started up the six by six, shoved it into reverse and backed out the way he had come. Once outside the gulag he turned the truck and gunned it forward, up the gentle slope.

O'Toole rode up front with him. Beck and Dr. Hatton were in the back, helping the prisoners as best they could.

"Tell the truth, Colonel," Liam said, "did you think we'd get this far?"

Barrabas shifted into a higher gear, picking up speed. "Yeah," he said. "This far."

23

Major Grabischenko answered the telephone on the twelfth ring. He answered it with a guttural growl.

"Is that you, Yevgeny?" said a familiar voice.

The GRU deputy chief sat bolt upright in bed. A surge of pure adrenaline blasted the sleep from his mind.

"Yevgeny, this is Viktor. Viktor Volkopyalov."

As Grabischenko had guessed.

"I am sorry to disturb you this late hour, but there has been some news from Ust Tavda, and I was certain you'd want to hear it as soon as possible."

"Yes?" he said, shutting his eyes.

"It seems your little Western entourage has disappeared."

Grabischenko's anger bubbled over. "Impossible!" he snapped. "They were guarded by fifteen of *spetsnaz*'s finest soldiers. There must be some mistake."

"Indeed," the KGB head said, the gloating in his voice unconcealed. "And the mistake I'm afraid is all yours."

"Yes?"

"They found your 'finest soldiers' about half an hour ago. They were all dead. And the people they were supposed to be guarding were gone."

"All dead!"

"No, I take that back. There was one survivor. Your friend, Captain Balandin."

Grabischenko breathed a sigh of relief.

It was short-lived.

"He did not escape unscathed, however," Volkopyalov said. "They castrated him."

The GRU man's heart stopped.

"There is more to tell, but my superiors feel you should be present to hear it. Don't make us come and get you. It's so undignified. Be in my office in twenty-five minutes."

The KGB head hung up.

Grabischenko just sat there, listening to the hum of the disengaged phone. It simply could not be true. It was some perverse game of Viktor's. If it was true, his life of privilege was over, his career ended in horrible disgrace.

He looked over at his pretty young wife sleeping peacefully beside him. How long would he keep her if he was exiled? Would she follow him to Siberia? He didn't like the answer he gave himself. No, that was being naive, anyway. They wouldn't send him to Siberia; they'd implicate him in some fictitious conspiracy against the state, execute him and bring down as many of his GRU cronies as they could.

He fought the panic rising in his throat. Think logically, he told himself. How good could KGB's information be? Ust Tavda was a long way from Moscow. Unless there was written confirmation or a statement by someone of impeccable reputation, KGB would not act. Perhaps they had caught wind of some small scandal and were trying to panic him into a free admission of a lesser crime. The result, his resignation, would be the same—only he would survive it.

Grabischenko slipped out of bed and began to get dressed. There had to be a rational explanation for what was happening. And he was going to find it.

24

Barrabas raced the truck right into the teeth of the KGB buzz saw. From well back of the stockade gates, the troops inside the main camp safely plugged away at the approaching truck.

Bullets sang off the cab roof, shot through the many jagged holes in the windshield, but neither the white-haired driver nor his red-haired passenger so much as flinched.

"You seem to be taking all this pretty calmly," Barrabas growled at O'Toole out of the corner of his mouth.

"Hey, Colonel, if there was any place to duck to, believe me I'd be ducking."

"Yeah, sure."

"We seem to be slowing up."

"Partially due to the grade, part to all the lead this heap has soaked up in the last half hour."

O'Toole stuck the muzzle of an AK out the side window and took some very casual offhand shots at the KGB men ahead. "They're too damn well protected," he said. "Can't see 'em, let alone hit 'em."

"The situation has its positive side, too. They're

so worried about joining their deceased comrades that they aren't aiming for shit.''

"Stop for a second," Liam said, putting down his AK and reloading the RPG. "I think I can hit the radio tower from here."

Barrabas slammed on the brakes, and O'Toole leaned out the open window. The rocket streaked away, four feet above the road, through the open gates. It smashed into the base of the tower and the low building that supported it. Building and tower went boom.

"The ultimate jammer," Liam said, pulling back inside.

Barrabas floored the accelerator, forcing the six by six to once again pick up speed. When he came to the airstrip turn, he cut the wheel hard over, presenting the truck's broadside momentarily to the guns of the main camp. "Everybody down back there!" he shouted over his shoulder. "Incoming!"

The KGB gunners hit the truck, all right. But most of the damage they did was to the canvas cover over the bed. Then Barrabas had them out of the fire lane and roaring full tilt down the hill to the airport.

"Looks like Billy and Chank had some trouble," O'Toole said.

Two figures stepped out from behind the crashed vehicles. One was tall, the other stout.

"Looks like they handled it," Barrabas said.

He pulled the truck up beside the wrecks.

"Sure glad to see your ugly face, O'Toole," Billy said. "Move the hell over and let's get out of here."

Liam obliged and the truck took on two more passengers. One Osage-Navaho in the front seat and one pure-blooded Inuit on the running board.

"Did you get him?" Billy asked. "Did you get the guy we came for?"

Barrabas nodded. He stopped the truck under the Ilyushin's open front door. "Everybody out! Billy, you and Chank give the others a hand in back."

Billy rounded the rear of the truck and threw back the canvas flaps. For a moment he was speechless. Then he recovered. "Who the hell are all these guys? Talk about down and out. Looks like we're opening our own salvation mission."

"That's about it," Lee said, helping one of the ambulatory prisoners of conscience to the tailgate. "We happen to be their only salvation. Let's get them into the plane as quickly and as carefully as we can. Some of them are in real bad way and they don't need any more rough treatment."

It wasn't such a hard job.

The five male mercenaries carried the prisoners in their arms, first to the side of the cab, then one at a time onto the truck hood, the roof, then gently passed them up to waiting hands at the plane's door. Lee saw to it that the newcomers were securely and comfortably fastened in their seats. She also kept a running tally on what appeared to be wrong with each of them and which cases were the most serious.

There were still three men to be lifted onto the hood when fresh gunfire from the camp on the hill erupted. It was from a heavy machine gun, like the kind that had fired on them from the gun towers.

It was also right on target.

Slugs skipped under the truck, glanced off the plane's landing gear struts and creased the aluminum underbelly of the fuselage.

The SOBs jumped down behind the protection of the truck.

The slim protection.

The machine gun was firing armor-piercing bullets.

"Look, Colonel," O'Toole said. "They've pulled the MG out of the gun tower we didn't hit and moved it out there in front of the gate."

"We can't take much of this," Beck said.

"There's one round of RPG left, Colonel," Billy Two said. "Let me take a crack at it."

"You've got the wrong tool, red man," Liam said. "There's no straight line from here to the MG. A rocket-propelled grenade has no trajectory. What you need is an M79 grenade launcher."

"Thanks for the information," Billy said. "We don't happen to have an M79. Colonel, I can get the right line if I work my way up the hill."

More slugs sailed past, pocking the side of the Ilyushin.

"Do it and do it quick!" Barrabas said.

The Indian gave a salute, hoisted the RPG out of

the truck cab and broke into a trot away from the plane and toward the camp.

Piece of cake, Billy told himself as he crossed the stretch of unprotected ground.

The men behind the MG let him get closer before they turned the gun on him. They knew something about angles, too.

Billy had his spot all picked out. It was only another thirty yards uphill. Then the MG chattered his way. Little chunks of ice and dirt jumped into the air all around him. The ground underfoot, even through the heavy soles of his snow boots, trembled under the hammering of all that steel-jacketed lead.

Billy had no choice. He couldn't outrun the fast-swinging muzzle. So he went down. They weren't going to let him get close enough to use the RPG. But he was determined to get off a shot, no matter what. He raised up on his elbows, shouldered the tube and fired. The rocket impacted high. It blew the top off the stockade fence above the MG position. At the very best it might have given the gun crew a few splinters. Cursing, the Indian turned and started to haul ass back to the plane. Something hot and huge hit his right calf. The impact flipped him on his butt and he slid to his back. He stayed down. It hurt. It hurt real bad.

"Aw, he's hit!" Beck said. "Billy's been hit!"

Barrabas squinted at the dark unmoving form. It was caught up in a maelstrom of bullet impacts.

"Son of a bitch!" he snarled, jumping down from the cab roof and sprinting for the fallen man.

The MG crew was waiting for something just like that.

They already had the range.

Slugs cut a line of death at the white-haired man's heels, forcing him to turn away, to turn back. "Bastards!" he raged.

Liam dived at the crouching leader, hitting him behind the knees, knocking him down as more bullets tracked his torso.

"Get off me, O'Toole," Barrabas shouted. "Nobody gets left behind. Nobody alive."

"We can't get to him."

"Get off me, or I'm gonna break your fucking neck!"

"Colonel, you're not thinking straight," Liam told him.

Beck slid to a stop beside them. "Doc put the binoculars on him," he said. "She says he's not breathing, and there's blood all over the place."

"She figures he's had it, too?" Barrabas asked.

"That's how she figures it."

More jacketed slugs shrieked over their heads and pinged into the silver skin of the Ilyushin.

"We've all had it if we hang around here any longer, Colonel," O'Toole said.

"Goddamnit, Liam, get off me!"

There was resignation in the white-haired man's voice. Resignation, anger and pain. His duty was to preserve the living as long as he could. Nile Barrabas never turned his back on duty.

O'Toole let him up.

"Get the last of the prisoners onto the plane," Barrabas said. "Let's get the hell out of here before somebody else buys a piece of this dump."

Chank watched the whole thing go down from the pilot's seat, tears streaming down his round cheeks. It was a reliving of his vision. Only he had interpreted it all wrong. Instead of seeing a premonition of his own death, he had previewed the death of his friend. His brown friend.

He was glad that it wasn't him and being glad made him ashamed. It was a natural, but unworthy thought.

Dayo wound the Ilyushin's engines to takeoff rpms. Maybe, he told himself, a man can never see his own death in advance. Maybe that is the one secret we are denied up until the last. The final joke with no audience to hear it.

He pushed the throttles forward and the plane surged ahead.

Rest in peace, old friend. In peace.

25

Grabischenko sat surrounded by his enemies. Hemmed in by more powerful men than he. The situation was grave, of that there could be no doubt. There was too much evidence mounting already. Statements from Ust Tavda.

And Volkopyalov was loving every minute of it.

"Perhaps this would be the right moment to inform Major Grabischenko of the new discovery?" the KGB man said.

There were nods around the oval table.

"It concerns the electronic device brought into our country by GRU's American friends."

"What about it?" Grabischenko said. "Isn't it operational?"

"Oh, yes, it appears to work as we were told."

"What then is the problem?"

"The problem is that your friends used the installation of the processor board as an excuse to get at our tank plant computer. In some way we have not yet ascertained, they have managed to shut the entire system down, to wipe the computer memory clean. The best guess is that our plant will be out of operation for six to eight months until the exact cause of the problem is located.''

"There, even you admit it!" the GRU man said. "You don't know the cause. This could all be coincidence. There is no proof. As there is no proof that the Americans killed anybody. It could have been our own people who did the killing. I don't need to remind you how many unpleasant deeds have been committed to further a man's rise to power.''

"Or wealth," Volkopyalov said. "How much did the United States pay for your help in sabotaging the Ust Tavda plant?''

"You are grasping at straws," the GRU man said. Sweat trickled down the hollow of his back. If there was a betrayal in the works, a man in Rio with ten million in diamonds was most certainly a part of it. "I wish to make a phone call overseas," Grabischenko said.

J. CRUIKSHANK KNEW a GRU man or men when he saw them. He also knew that if they wanted to see him, a locked door would be no deterrent.

He stepped back from the hotel door's peephole and tightened the sash on his silk bathrobe, then he unlocked the door.

"Yes, gentlemen, what can I do for you?"

Both the GRU men were stamped from the same mold: crew-cut, medium-brown hair, stocky, powerfully built, dressed in cheap tropical-weight suits. They pushed past him into the suite.

"There has been a problem with your product," one of the men said. "My employers want to enforce the guarantee. They want their diamonds back."

Cruikshank paled. "Now, wait a minute," he said, waving his long thin arms. "Before I return the diamonds I want to verify that my product is really defective. To do that I must see it."

"That is impossible. Where are the diamonds?"

"Look here, I've done business with your Major Grabischenko before. Surely he isn't aware of. . . ."

"We are acting under the major's orders. The diamonds, now, and quickly, please, or we will use force."

Cruikshank knew of GRU's handiwork when it came to obtaining information from reluctant parties. He had no interest in losing an eye or a kidney, or in having his spleen ruptured, no matter how much money was involved. The whole thing was undoubtedly some kind of misunderstanding. The Soviets damn well needed him. And they would come around.

"They're in the wall safe behind the mirror," he said.

"Open it."

Cruikshank slid the mirror aside and rotated the safe's knob. When the tumblers clicked he stepped back.

"I said open it," the GRU man repeated. "Open it and step back."

Cruikshank did as he was told.

The other GRU man took out the case with the diamonds in it. He opened it and looked inside.

"The stones are all there?"

"Yes, certainly," Cruikshank said.

"Good."

The man with the case closed it. Then he and his partner took hold of the entrepreneur's skinny arms.

"No! What is this!" Cruikshank protested as he was dragged to the sliding glass door that opened onto his balcony.

"I understand you have a wonderful view," the GRU man said.

Cruikshank fought with all his strength when he realized what was in store for him.

All his squirming and thrashing amounted to nothing. And when he started to scream, the two men hoisted him over the edge of the balcony.

Cruikshank got his scream out, then. It was a dilly. And it lasted exactly nineteen stories.

26

By no stretch of the imagination could the Ilyushin II-14 be considered "fast." It was, in fact, infuriatingly slow. It crept over the Urals, then due west at a steady two hundred miles per hour. The closer the SOBs got to their goal, the slower their progress seemed and the more nervous everyone became.

Four and a half hours had passed without contact, without challenge or sign of pursuit. It was too good to be true.

Barrabas glared out the front windscreen from the copilot's seat. Dayo couldn't have flown the plane any lower without putting them in the treetops. He couldn't have flown a straighter course, either. There hadn't been any point in trying to completely avoid Leningrad by swinging south around it. Barrabas knew there were TU-126 Soviet AWACS patrolling in the neighborhood. Tactical nerve centers that could call in ground-to-air missiles or the airborne border defenses, the SU-15A and TU-28 interceptors. The SOBs' only real hope had been to get out of Russian airspace as quickly as possible, before news of what they had done leaked out.

Surely the news was out by now.

"What do you think, Colonel?" Liam asked.

"I don't know," the white-haired man said. They crawled toward the Gulf of Finland, a band of silvery gray on the horizon. To the east, the sky was growing light.

"There's only one explanation," Nate Beck told them.

"And it ain't dumb luck," Dayo cut in.

"And it ain't your flying, as good as it is," Barrabas said. The tendons of his jaw flexed as he gritted his teeth. "Somebody down there likes us. The best air-defense system in the world doesn't make the same mistake for five hours. We've been given a free pass out."

"After what we've done?!" Liam said.

Barrabas scowled. "What have we done? And who've we done it for? I thought I knew. Now I'm not so sure."

"If we make it out," Liam said, "it's going to embarrass the hell out of a lot of bigwigs...."

"That's right," Beck said. "It'll shake up the hierarchies of both Soviet intelligence services. A lot of the most powerful men will lose their jobs, not to mention their heads. It'll make room at the top for others. Younger, more ambitious, even more ruthless."

"In other words," O'Toole said, "we've been

had from square one. Jerked around like goddamn puppets.''

"Not necessarily," Barrabas told him. "It's more likely that we just happened along with the right stuff at the right time. Whoever's letting us go was ready to seize the opportunity our little enterprise offered.''

The Ilyushin left the Russian mainland behind, heading due north across the gulf for the coast of Finland.

"We're gonna make it," Dayo said as they crossed the midpoint of the gulf, the boundary to freedom.

"We might have made it, but it doesn't look so good for Leonov," Dr. Hatton said, leaning into the cabin. "On top of his chest injury and the infection, he's badly frostbitten.''

"Has he regained consciousness?" Barrabas asked.

"He's delirious from the fever. Raving. I've got nothing to sedate him with.''

"Do what you can for him," Barrabas told her. "It won't be long now. Once we land in Helsinki, it'll all be out of our hands.''

Lee shook her head. "Nile, it's already out of our hands.''

27

Weak winter daylight streamed in through the window to Grabischenko's left, illuminating the confident faces of his enemies as they shuffled bits of paper and shared whispered secrets. It had been a long, terrible night of accusations, counteraccusations, thrusts and parries. A long lonely night. He had been cut off from his own organization, from his personal information sources, from potential scapegoats, left to dangle by himself from KGB's sturdy scaffold. His exhaustion, physical and mental, was nearly total. Cups of strong coffee no longer had any effect on him. And the ordeal was not over yet.

Viktor Volkopyalov hung up a secure telephone, the corners of his mouth twitching as he fought to control the urge to smile broadly, openly in the face of his one-time friend.

"Gentlemen," the KGB deputy head said, "we have further news."

All eyes turned toward the squat well-dressed man.

"A Mayday call was logged in at 23:52 hours last

night," Volkopyalov said. "It was transmitted only once. It came from our stolen aircraft."

"Then they crashed?" Grabischenko asked.

Volkopyalov could not control his smile any longer. "No, they landed," he said. "They set down on an airstrip next to the Tarkotovo gulag."

The GRU man gave him a doubtful look.

"Using automatic weapons and rocket-propelled grenades of Soviet manufacture, they staged a successful attack on the main camp, murdering most of the prison staff."

"Soviet weapons!" Grabischenko exclaimed. "Where did they get their hands on—"

"KGB's question, precisely," Volkopyalov interrupted.

Grabischenko's face burned with suppressed fury. They were giving him the shaft, all right. Every inch of it. "And the purpose of this attack?" he said.

"As my colleagues are aware," the KGB head said, "there is a satellite camp close to the main Tarkotovo gulag. A special-regime colony. One of the politicals imprisoned there was Anatoly Leonov...."

"Was?" Grabischenko croaked.

Volkopyalov nodded. "Your mercenaries attacked the satellite camp as well, freeing a number of prisoners of conscience, among them one of our most distinguished dissidents."

"They couldn't have gotten away," Grabischenko said. "Surely, they were shot down by our border defenses."

The look in his former friend's eyes told him everything.

"You let them go, you bastard!" Grabischenko snarled. "I'll bet you didn't even scramble the interceptors. Bastard! You probably opened a clear lane for them the entire way out."

"Regrettably it was too late to take action against them," Volkopyalov said. "If you had come forward earlier and confessed your crimes, we could have prevented their escape. It was your cowardice that allowed them to succeed."

"I confess nothing! I have done nothing!"

The assembled KGB heads held a short conference, then Volkopyalov addressed him in a formal manner, the manner of a judge laying down a death sentence.

"You will return to your home under guard. You will stay there until you are called for trial. You will be allowed no contact with any member of GRU. You may leave."

Grabischenko exited the room on legs of wood. An escort of armed KGB men walked him out of the building and saw that he got into his limousine. He sank back on the soft cushions as his driver pulled away from the curb. There were KGB cars ahead and behind.

It was over.

His years of service, of effort, of sacrifice all for

nothing. Volkopyalov and the others had him cold. They would connect him with the weapons, the planning, everything. He would become the mastermind of the whole enterprise. Put on public display for public humiliation. For public amusement. And every day that the trial dragged on, every hour, the GRU would be held up to further shame.

Grabischenko managed a dry laugh. KGB had made a mistake when they transferred him to their weak sister. His allegiance had been transferred as well. Even though his own career was beyond hope, he still had it in his power to ease the damage his downfall would cause the GRU.

He rapped lightly on the glass panel that separated the limousine's passenger compartment from the chauffeur. The driver looked up in his rearview mirror and lowered the power window.

"Pavel," Grabischenko said, "give me your pistol."

The chauffeur reached inside his jacket and produced a Stechkin 9mm automatic that he passed through the open window.

"Close the window," Grabischenko said.

There was no point in putting it off.

The moment the driver shut the window, Grabischenko cocked the pistol's slide. He did it twice, ejecting one live round, making sure there was another under the firing pin. He closed his eyes and pushed the muzzle of the Stechkin into his mouth. The bitter taste of gun oil assaulted his tongue. Then he pulled the trigger.

28

"It's coming on now," Jessup said as he adjusted the volume on the television set.

Nile Barrabas looked up from the straight Scotch on the rocks he was pouring for himself. The face that filled the nineteen-inch screen belonged to the newly freed Soviet dissident, Anatoly Leonov. Barrabas rounded the bar of the South Kensington flat for a closer look.

As he did so, the man on the screen opened his mouth and began to address a rapt global audience. The sounds that escaped the scientist's lips were startling. Not words, not sentences, sounds.

Animal sounds.

Inarticulate expressions of horror.

"Oh, God," Jessup said softly.

Perhaps in some tiny sane corner of his mind Leonov realized he was raving because he tried harder, more desperately to communicate. The result was frenzy. Piercing shrieks. Wild hand gestures. His eyes streamed endless tears.

"Those fucking bastards!" Jessup snarled. "They couldn't wait to parade him, to show off their trophy! Their symbol of freedom! It's like a sideshow. A freak show.''

Barrabas stared at the electronic image of a face in torment. He heard the helpless, hopeless laughter of the TV crew as the great, the brilliant, the indomitable disintegrated before their eyes. Leonov screamed into the camera, his open mouth covering the screen. He was drooling like an infant.

For this the SOBs had gone to hell and back.

For this William Starfoot II had given up his life.

Barrabas grabbed the quart bottle of Scotch from the bar top. ''Enough!'' he shouted as he threw the bottle through the TV screen. ''Enough!''

29

When Billy Two awoke he was in a white room. On his back in a white bed. He tried to move and could not. His right leg was in a heavy plaster cast that ran from ankle to hip. That wasn't what was keeping him down, though.

It was the straps.

Across his chest, his middle, his legs.

Thick leather straps buckled to the bed frame.

He tried to move against them, to test them, but he was too weak. The slight exertion made his face break out in a sweat. He felt like he was going to pass out.

When his head cleared, he tried to remember what had happened to him, what had put him flat on his back in a hospital bed. The harder he tried to recall things, the further away they seemed to slip and then the dizziness returned and he thought he was going to be sick.

I must be medicated up the yang, he told himself after the vertigo had passed. Nobody is this screwed up in the head from a busted leg.

The door to his room opened inward, and a hospital orderly in a gray uniform entered carrying a stainless-steel tray. On the tray was a pad of cotton, a small bottle of pink liquid and a hypodermic syringe.

"Hey, buddy," Billy Two said. "I don't need that anymore. I've come around. On my way to recovery. I don't need the straps anymore, either. I'm not going to fall out of the bed."

The orderly ignored him, set the tray down on a white enamel table and proceeded to load the syringe.

"Hey, didn't you hear me?" Billy said. "The dope is not required."

The orderly advanced on him, a wad of cotton in one hand and the hypo in the other.

Billy struggled against the straps. "No, you dumb son of a bitch! I want the doctor! The doctor!"

The needle sank into his forearm.

As the orderly depressed the plunger, he said something to Billy.

"What?" the Indian said.

As the man withdrew the needle he repeated what he had said.

Billy didn't understand him any better the second time, but at least he knew what the problem was. The guy was talking Russian.

It was the key that opened all the doors.

Memory returned in a staggering rush.

A rush equal to the drug surge melting his brain.

"Oh, shit," Billy Two groaned, then the white room went black.

Update on Jack Hild

Dear Editors,

I got a real boot out of your request in the back of SOBs #3, asking to hear from anyone who claimed to have seen Jack Hild. Hell, I'd like to hear from them, too. You see, I know for a fact that Jack Hild is dead. Has been dead for three years. I know because I buried him in the bush in Zambia, dug the hole with my own two hands.

Did Jack suffer in his passing? Hell, no. He was two-thirds crocked on native hooch when we got jumped by guys in uniform. They didn't ask any questions; they just opened up with autorifles. I survived only because there was so much blood splattered on me the bastards thought I was dead, too.

I don't know where you're digging up Jack's books. And they are definitely his. There's no mistaking his writing. The "eat the rat" scene in SOBs #3, *Butchers of Eden*, is a goddamn classic. It really happened, too. I know because I told him the story. Old Jack borrowed freely from his running buddies... money, women *and* ideas.

I just wanted to set the record straight.

Like Jack used to say...

Vafan,

R.S., Captain, U.S.M.C., Ret.

More on Jack Hild

Dear Editors,

Jack Hild is a son of a bitch!

I know because I have met him. The first time was in Paris on the evening of 23 July, 1983. A friend of a friend suggested he contact me regarding some background information for a book on Iran he was writing. He seemed an educated man, polite, even charming. I accepted him into my home, answered his many questions about my native land, and over the course of a few days he led me to believe he was sympathetic to the cause of Khomeini. When I saw the book he wrote, SOBs #2, *The Plains of Fire*, I was shocked. Jack Hild twisted everything I told him. He made my country's leaders seem like soulless, cowardly murderers.

Jack Hild is the coward! And your company should be condemned for printing such obvious lies.

B.H.-T., Paris, 27 November 1984

P.S.: Though she denies it, I know he made love with my wife.

**Nile Barrabas and the
Soldiers of Barrabas are the**

by Jack Hild

Nile Barrabas is a nervy son of a bitch who was the last
American soldier out of Vietnam and the first man into a
new kind of action. His warriors, called the Soldiers of
Barrabas, have one very simple ambition: to do what the
Marines can't or won't do. Join the Barrabas blitz! Each
book hits new heights—this is brawling at its best!

#1 The Barrabas Run   **#4 Show No Mercy**
#2 The Plains of Fire   **#5 Gulag War**
#3 Butchers of Eden

GOLD
EAGLE

Available wherever paperbacks are sold.